MAKING MAGIC

MAKING MAGIC

THE WITCHES OF PRESSLER STREET™ BOOK TWO

MARTHA CARR

MICHAEL ANDERLE

THE MAKING MAGIC TEAM

To the Early Readers Team
Kathleen Fettig
Michael Robbins
Debi Sateren
Michael Baumann

Special shout out to Grace Snokes, Lynne Stiegler, Judah
Raine, Kelly O'Donnell and Stephen Campbell for their
general badassery behind the scenes to keep everything
running so smoothly.

From Martha

To all those who love to read, and like a good puzzle inside
a good story
To Michael Anderle for his generosity
to all his fellow authors
To Louie and Jackie
And in memory of my big sister,
Dr. Diana Deane Carr
who first taught me about magic, Star Trek,
DC Comics and flaming cherries jubilee

From Michael

To Family, Friends and
Those Who Love
To Read.
May We All Enjoy Grace
To Live The Life We Are
Called.

CHAPTER ONE

"Are you kidding me? A five-year-old could draw a better map than this." Laura Hadstrom turned the piece of paper sideways, upside-down, and back to what she thought was right-side up. "Okay, maybe that five-year-old was me. But still. Dad didn't even put a compass in the corner…"

Her hand reflexively went to her back pocket, but she stopped. "Right. Left my wand at home because, apparently, we don't need them anymore." Squinting at her dad's crudely drawn map, she tilted her head to see it better beneath the dim glow of a 12th Street West streetlight.

The moment she wanted more light, the silver ring on her thumb—her own physical piece of the Hadstrom family legacy—flashed, and her dad's map glowed from within, a single point on it illuminated brighter than the rest. "*There* we go. Next time, I'm gonna tell him to at least put a big star or something so I know where to start." Laura glanced at her ring. "Wonder if my sisters have figured out how to use their rings better than the wands."

With a shrug, she looked at the back of the Bullock Texas State History Museum. "Okay. Ten-thirty at night. Doors are locked. Lights are off. If there's anybody watching…guess I'll just cross that bridge later." She walked along the long stretch of the museum's back wall until she got to what could have been the illuminated spot on the map—if her dad had drawn anything to scale. But she didn't see anything. No back door, no shed, no outbuilding. Shaking her head, Laura puffed out a sigh, then glanced at her ring. "Let's try again."

She tapped the illuminated space on the map, then pointed at the back of the museum and drew her finger through the air like she would have with her wand. "*Ostendo.*" The same muted glow rose from her ring, moved through her pointing finger, and shot out toward the building. "Hey." She grinned at the ring. "I think we're starting to get to know each other. Now where is it?"

For a few seconds, she thought she'd missed the mark, then her gaze fell to the asphalt of the employee parking lot. A circle of muted light pulsed on the ground. Laura wrinkled her nose. "Why does it have to be a manhole?" With a sigh, she folded the map, stuck it in her wand-less back pocket, and headed toward the glowing manhole cover.

She glanced around to be sure no one was watching, then whispered, "*Patentibus.*"

The silver ring flashed brighter, and the glowing metal disk set in the asphalt jumped from its place over the manhole and tossed itself two feet to the side. The loud *clang* echoed against the building and over the parking lot as the cover spun several times like a wobbly top before coming to a stop. "Okay, so there's still a learning curve. That was way stronger than I wanted."

After a few seconds of listening for a warning shout or footsteps headed toward her—and only hearing the buzzing insects in the summer heat, even at night, plus a yowling cat a few blocks away—Laura stepped toward the gaping black hole.

"Down the rabbit hole, then." She pointed into the blackness. Before she could utter the spell she'd always had to say with her wand, her ring summoned a bubble of soft light that beamed down into the darkness. Laura blinked away her surprise, then smirked and turned around to lower herself onto the now-visible rebar serving as ladder rungs.

The glowing light moved as she moved, illuminating a radius five feet around her. "Man, this thing goes down forever. Like the time I went through those caves up north." She chuckled. "I thought I was never gonna reach the bottom, then *bam*. There I was, right where that eighth-century potion's bowl had been hanging out for five hundred years without ever—oh!" Her right foot missed the next rung, and she realized it was gone.

Laura wobbled on the rebar ladder and tightened her grip. "Pay attention." She peered down and saw the ground three feet beneath her, so she steadied herself and dropped nimbly the rest of the way.

When she stood, Laura found herself in a concrete cavern with three branching tunnels on the far end. She fetched her dad's map out to check which way the first arrow pointed. "Okay, standing here...yep. We're going with the right tunnel." The light followed her across the cavern and into the tunnel on the right, which narrowed around her until she felt too big for the tiny passage. "It's like *Charlie and the Chocolate Factory* down here," she muttered. "There's no way I can keep going."

Then she spied steps at the end of the tunnel. Metal grates led down one step at a time. Laura moved slowly down, taking care not to hit her head on the low ceiling.

"Now *this* looks like a ship."

The incredibly large room before her descended hundreds of feet into the darkness; even her trailing bubble of light couldn't reach the bottom. The grated stairs led right to a narrow catwalk stretching across the gaping hole. On the other side, she discerned a storage room without any walls or railings. Four more grated staircases descended through the nothingness toward other platforms at various levels. Ropes and nets hung from every metal beam and pillar, creating a lattice that gave the illusion of enclosed walls—only she could see everything through the nets.

"Good thing I'm not afraid of heights." Laura cocked her head and set off across the catwalk toward the first platform on the other side. Her footsteps echoed through so much space, and she leaned over the side to try to glimpse the bottom. "Nothing." With a nod, she walked the other half of the grated catwalk and stepped onto a wide, circular, concrete platform. A huge metal column stretched from the platform to the ceiling of the cavern, though even that was too far above to see. Boxes, metal crates, dusty tarps, more draped netting, and a collection of unfamiliar metal tools lay strewn about without any rhyme or reason. Laura lifted her foot when she made out something soft beneath her shoe. It looked like...a pelt?

"What kinda place *is* this?"

The map came out again, and she turned it every which way to orient herself. She squinted up the metal column and took a few more steps forward. "Hello?" She hadn't raised her voice that much, but with the echo she might as well have shouted.

Dad said she lives here. I think he forgot the facts about this just like everyone in the world forgot how to lock the Gorafrex back up in its prison...

"My name's Laura Hadstrom," she called. Her name echoed back a dozen times. "My father Gregory Hadstrom told me I would find you here, that you might be able to help with a little Gorafrex problem."

She took a few more steps across the platform, then stopped to listen for a response. "Come on," Laura whispered. "This can't just be another dead end—"

Beside the metal column, a pile of tarps shifted. Then it rose at the center, all the material shifting and sliding around. A few scattered newspaper pages slipped out and fluttered to the floor, and the pile grew and grew. It looked like a massive bear rising out of hibernation, though covered in canvas instead of fur. Laura stared as all the tarps slid away.

The Engineer might have been nine feet tall if she wasn't bent over with age; as it was, she hunched at around seven feet. A huge mop of tangled gray curls fell to her shoulders, partially hiding the dirty, wrinkled face beneath. The giant woman shook the hair out of her eyes, which glistened huge and bug-like in her face, then Laura realized she wore some kind of magnifying goggles. *Or really thick glasses...* The woman's jumpsuit was a patchwork collection of tan, dark-green, and faded copper, covered in zippered pockets and straps and buckles. Those huge eyes behind the goggles blinked slowly, and the Engineer took a shuffling step forward. Laura felt the concrete platform shudder, but she stood her ground.

The Engineer caught sight of her and craned her neck forward, squinting. "You are so loud," the old woman said, her voice deep and coarse with age and infrequent use. "I could hear you all the way from the surface."

"Oh." Laura smiled and gave a little shrug. "Sorry about that. My name's—"

"Laura Hadstrom. Yes, I know." The Engineer turned away from Laura and took another shuffling step in the other direction. "I haven't heard the Gorafrex mentioned in eons. Why are you coming to me about this?"

"Well...I—"

The Engineer's huge hand came slapping down with incredible speed onto one of the metal crates in front of her. When she lifted it again, she'd caught something that looked an awful lot like a cockroach three times bigger than Laura thought they should ever be allowed to grow. And that brown, glistening bug went into the Engineer's mouth with a loud crunch.

Ew. Laura swallowed. She forced herself to speak through the crunch and wet smack of the bug between the Engineer's teeth. "I came to you because my sisters and I need your help."

"Is there such a shortage of knowledge these days?" A

glob of something thick and yellow dribbled down the woman's wrinkled lip.

Laura's nostrils flared, and she pulled her gaze up to the Engineer's magnified eyes behind the goggles. "It definitely seems that way. Yes."

The woman swallowed with a loud *glurp*. "And you came to me for such knowledge of the Gorafrex. *Why?*" That last word was a harsh, hissing whisper.

Better go with the truth this time. It'll come out anyway.

Laura took a deep breath. "Because, well…I *accidentally* set it free."

CHAPTER TWO

The Engineer blinked her huge eyes behind the giant goggles. Quicker than seemed possible, the giant of an old woman stormed toward Laura. The entire platform shook with every massive step, sending items and papers toppling from the piles of crates. A few loose wires and heavy rope nets laden with all kinds of odds and ends broke free beneath the force of the Engineer's movement. The old woman stopped in front of Laura, blocking out almost all the light, and loomed over her. "*Your* ancestors put that creature away to protect this ship and everyone on it!" Her roaring voice echoing through the cavern brought a few sheets of dust falling down all around them. "Why would you let it *out*? You foolish child!"

Laura stood her ground, craning her neck to meet the Engineer's bug-like eyes. "I didn't know." She said it calmly and evenly enough. "I found the prison in the Greenbelt, and I wanted to find out what was behind those wards. I didn't figure it out until *after* the Gorafrex escaped it was a prison, or that the Gorafrex was what came out of it, or even that my family are the ones responsible for keeping it locked up."

The Engineer hissed down at her, then stopped abruptly. Her large eyes flickered down to Laura's hand and the silver ring on her thumb. "Your family. Yes." She straightened, took one step back, and gave Laura enough space to breathe again. "And they told you everything you needed to know when you received that channeling trinket you wear, hm?"

"Well, not exactly." Laura glanced at the ring. "My sisters and I got our rings from our dad. And he told us about the Gorafrex. Why it's here, what it wants, and why my ancestors made that prison." The Engineer grunted. "He told us what *he* knew, but it's not everything we need to put that thing back before it..." *I have to talk about this, don't I? We need this woman's help.*

"Before it consumes the body of a human? Before it kills a witch or wizard? Before it fully escapes this ship and takes us all down with it?"

Okay, I definitely didn't expect us to go down that road. "The first two have already happened," Laura said. "I don't want them to happen again, if I can do anything about it. And I definitely don't want it to get to the whole escaping-the-ship part—wait. Can you clarify that one for me?"

"Can I—" The Engineer took another step back, cocked her head, then threw it back toward the black, gaping chasm above them and let out a shrill, dusty-sounding cackle.

Laura pressed her lips together and waited for the woman to finish. *We are dealing with some serious mood swings, aren't we?*

Finally, the Engineer hunched over again and fell into dry chuckles. "Oh, Laura Hadstrom. You are *so* young. It is very endearing, you know."

"Well, I'm glad you think so...um...I'm sorry, I didn't get your name."

"You may call me Rutilda." The Engineer shuffled back toward the stacked crates and slumped her massive behind down on the tarps covering them. A huge puff of dust shot out beneath her, and she rubbed her large hands up and down her thighs over the mottled green jumpsuit. "Come sit. Make yourself comfortable, Laura Hadstrom. I shall *clarify* for you."

"All right. Thank you." Laura moved farther onto the platform, taking care to step around the various tools and coiled cables and odd implements that had scattered across the floor at Rutilda's outburst. She found what looked like a footlocker just in front of the Engineer and used it as a chair—since there definitely weren't any chairs down here.

"It's clear you know that the stone above the surface is a door into the Gorafrex's prison," the old woman began. "One of many doors, yes, but all the others have long been thoroughly sealed. Not so easy for any being to get much farther into the bowels of this ship. Unless one is an Engineer like myself. Or one of the Mechanics."

"You mean the Huldu?" Laura had met only a few of the short magical gnomes, who spent a lot less time in the world above than their more human-looking cousins. "And the Kashgar?"

"Yes. Those." Ratilda bowed her head. "Just like them, a number of my people helped to build this ship. We set out on its maiden voyage and looked to the stars for our next destination." A loud sigh escaped her. "No one expected us to end up so far off course, orbiting for millennia around *this* star."

"Yeah, I've heard *this* story." Laura pressed her lips together and waited for the Engineer's reaction. *Don't push her too hard, Laura. You still need her help.*

"It's all the same story, Laura Hadstrom." Ratilda sucked a bit of giant cockroach from between her teeth. "One very long, very tedious story, in the end. But everything is connected. It's been ages since I've told or heard a story, mind you. All the other Velikan, my people, have since given themselves to the dust and the darkness of the vessel we created. I am the very last. Unless another snuck aboard the ship and hasn't come to visit once in billions of years." Ratilda chuckled again, sucked in a deep breath, and flicked her sharp gaze toward the witch sitting in front of her. "If I want to tell a bit of a story, Laura Hadstrom, I'll tell it."

"Right." Laura nodded. *No wonder she's losing her mind. Ancient and all alone down here.* "Please continue." She fought the urge to look at her Expedition watch.

"Yes. I will continue." The Velikan closed her eyes for a moment. "Yes. The Gorafrex prison was not a part of this ship's original design, you understand? When the first Hadstroms of your line discovered the creature had stolen aboard, thirsting for the magic of *your* kind, Laura Hadstrom—the magic of witches and wizards—to sustain it, your ancestors came to me and mine. They asked us for help in building that prison, and we obliged."

Laura nodded, working hard to keep her mouth shut. *When is she going to get to the point already? I know this stuff.*

"But capturing a creature as powerful as a Gorafrex and keeping it aboard with all the other passengers—a good portion of whom it wanted to kill, dissect, and consume, mind you..." Ratilda chuckled and shook her head. "That does not leave good marks on the history of a vessel's maiden voyage. And it makes people very tense."

Laura smirked. *No kidding.*

"So we devised a secondary purpose for the prison. A default plan, if you will." The Engineer lifted her great, gnarled hands and stared at the space between them. "The prison would contain the Gorafrex. And all around it, we built..." She took a deep, excited breath. "Another ship." The woman's aged lips peeled back into a grin, and she studied Laura with those bug-like eyes behind the goggles. She waited for the young witch to share her enthusiasm.

"Another...ship?"

"Yes. It was rather clever. I designed it myself, which I'm sure you've already guessed. And we built it with your ancestors to use when this ship crossed the empty wastes between the galaxy of our former home, Arenya V, and the quite distant sector of our destination. The thing was beautiful. A true testament to—"

"Why would you build a ship around a prison?" Laura frowned at the Engineer then realized her mistake. *Whoops. She's still in story mode.*

The Engineer's brow descended and folded over the tops of her goggles.

"I'm sorry. I—"

"To get the Gorafrex *off* this ship! To eject it into the barren wastelands of space between galaxies and let it live out its days alone, unfed, undying, unsatisfied. To eliminate the *threat.*" The woman overly annunciated the 't' sounds with her last sentence.

Kinda sounds like she's threatening me. "Like an escape pod."

Rutilda blinked slowly. "That is very rudimentary, Laura Hadstrom, but yes. If that allows you to better comprehend the complexities of this impromptu creation, it was something like…an escape pod."

"Built around the prison?"

"Yes."

"Here in Austin, Texas?"

The old Engineer glanced around the cavernous expanse underground. "Unless some idiot has uprooted the entire city above the surface and placed it somewhere else, then yes. Right here in what you quaintly call 'Austin.'"

Laura squinted. "Okay…so why didn't you…*eject* it? It's still here. The first Hadstrom witches locked the Gorafrex away in the prison, and…then what? Everybody thought they'd just keep it around a little longer? See what happens?"

Rutilda slid her hands down her thighs toward her knees and leaned toward the young witch. "Child, I realize it is difficult for you to understand the passage of time in the same way us long-lived races experience it. You get a century and a half and call it a lifetime. Maybe two centuries, if you're lucky. Everything must always be done so quickly with your species."

"A few billion years is a *really* long time to push the red button and shoot the Gorafrex off this ship, though. I mean, seriously." Laura tossed her thumb sideways in a crude miming of the only way she'd seen escape pods work, which was in sci-fi movies.

"Again, *very* rudimentary." The Engineer sighed. "The ship we built around that prison, like everything that keeps this ship running despite its never-ending orbital repetition"—Rutilda jerked her finger around in quick, exaggerated circles, rolling her eyes—"requires a highly sophisticated, advanced technological magic to power it in any way. And this smaller vessel, because it was not of the larger ship's original design, required a significant amount of magic. Yes, we could have brought together all the passengers and invited them to power the Gorafrex's *escape pod* with us. And then what would have been left for us to deal with? A ship full of panicked, enraged, resentful travelers who would spend more time sussing out tiny details like *how the Gorafrex snuck on board* in the first place rather than focusing on powering the energy cores—" A fit of dry, hacking coughs overwhelmed the old woman, and it took her a moment to stop first so she could catch her breath.

"Are you okay?" Laura asked. "Do you have a…giant vat of water around here or something?"

Rutilda chuckled and shook her head. "Such a funny creature you are, Laura Hadstrom. Ha. Water…"

It wasn't supposed to be funny, but okay. Again, the young witch fought the urge to look at her watch. *It's gotta be at least midnight by now. At least Nicki and Emily aren't waiting up for me or anything. 'Cause I didn't actually tell my sisters I was coming down here...*

CHAPTER THREE

"Now." The Engineer took a deep, rattling breath, and paused. "Where was I?"

"Um…" Laura blinked. "It took a lot of magic to power the energy cores?"

"Yes, yes. This ship was meant as a sanctuary. A safe place to deliver lifeforms across the universe to a new life elsewhere. Adventurers, businessfolk, refugee witches and wizards. We could not tell everyone that one of the most powerful beings we'd seen on Arenya V, bent on hunting down your kind, was trapped aboard with the rest of us. So the Engineers, Mechanics, and your ancestors, Laura Hadstrom, decided to take our time. We endeavored to fill each of the energy cores with a bit of magic at a time, so as not to exhaust ourselves or draw undue attention to the prison. Time…ha. We thought we had so much more of it."

Oh. Now I get it. "But the ship malfunctioned." Laura puffed out a sigh. "And we barreled right for this solar system."

"And here we remain." Rutilda lifted her hands in exasperation and dropped them to her thighs again with a puff of more dust. "We could not unleash the Gorafrex within this galaxy. That would put too many other systems and planets and lives at risk, so we stopped powering the new vessel. We waited for the necessary repairs. Which, somehow, became impossible to complete…"

"And the Gorafrex just stayed where it was."

"And it remained. Yes. But it knows, Laura Hadstrom. The creature knows what we planned, and it knows what the prison was made to do. Now that *you* have released it"—Laura grimaced—"it can, for the first time, access the energy cores it has spent the last few billion years coveting."

"It wants witches and wizards…*and* it wants to shoot itself into space?"

"And why not? To free itself from its captors and find a new system with inhabited planets. More witches. More prey. In a place where absolutely no one yet knows it has come for them."

"Boy." Laura rubbed her face and closed her eyes. *That makes things a little more complicated.* "Do you know how to stop the Gorafrex? How to capture it again and put it back in the prison?"

"Hmm." The Engineer tilted her head and stared into the darkness. "I heard pure iron was useful. And something about music…"

"Right. We already know about those. Just haven't figured out how to use them the right way."

"Well, I'm an Engineer, Laura Hadstrom. I know how to build and create and design these wondrous and infuriatingly unpredictable ships. And you are…well, you are a

Hadstrom witch. I imagine you and your...sisters, did you say?" Laura nodded. "You are responsible for figuring out the witches' work." Rutilda spread her arms with a shrug.

"Yeah. I know that too."

"Until you *do* figure it out, I suggest you and your sisters turn your focus to this abandoned *escape pod* of mine. And to be clear, I really do hate that term."

Laura cocked her head. "What do *you* call it?"

"A ship."

"Okay...but we don't know anything about energy cores or powering ships—"

"No!" Rutilda's shout echoed violently through the expansive cavern. "No, Laura Hadstrom. *You* are never to power that ship. No one should ever power it."

I think this woman might've actually lost her mind. "But... you just said to turn our focus to the escape pod."

"Not to *turn it on*. Oh, of all the idiotic..." The Engineer snorted and shook her head, her gray curls flying in all directions. "That ship has been there far too long. If anyone powers it, it will level the land all around for a great distance. Everything you know—every*one* you know—*poof*. And if the Gorafrex activates it, forget about your city. Or the realm you call the United States. Or any so-called continents. That ship would blast a massive hole in this ship and take all of us with it. And not as prisoners, Laura Hadstrom. As corpses."

Laura took a deep breath and folded her hands in her lap. "Oh." *Yeah. A lot more complicated.*

"What you need is to dismantle the energy cores. You and your sisters must destroy the ship I built around that prison, so the Gorafrex may never use it to *fully* escape.

Then, lock that creature away and be sure the Hadstroms of the future *never* have to find out about it the way you did, hmm?"

"Yeah. This *is* a learning opportunity for everybody."

Rutilda let out another wheezing, dusty cackle. "You *are* funny."

"Thanks…" Laura stood from the footlocker and nodded. "So how do we find these energy cores?"

"By looking for them, of course."

The young witch blinked and held her tongue. *Not helpful. At least I've had so much practice learning to ask questions in a million different ways. Wow. Never thought I'd be thanking Gilroy, of all magical artifacts…* "Okay. And *where* do we look?"

"Ah. It's very simple, really. The heart of the prison is also the heart of that ship. The very center." The Engineer lifted her wrinkled fingers again to slowly draw in the air. "Twelve energy cores arranged in a very large circle. I believe most of your Austin, Texas falls within that perimeter—"

"Wait." Laura whipped her phone out of her back pocket and pulled up the photo she'd taken a few days before. The sight of all the blood drawn upon the wall of that poor awakened peabrain's house in South Austin—the blood of the first and only witch, so far, that the Gorafrex had killed—made her pause. She stepped toward the Engineer and held up her phone, which she realized was incredibly small for the giant, ancient woman. "Is this what the escape pod looks like?"

"Eh? What's that?"

"It's a picture—"

"In your hand. What is it?"

Laura blinked. "Oh. It's a...cell phone. You know, for calling people. Yeah, *and* for taking pictures. It does a lot of stuff, actually. But that's not really important. Can you see the symbol in this picture?"

Rutilda squinted through her magnifying goggles and craned her neck forward. "My eyes aren't what they used to be, Laura Hadstrom."

"Okay, here." Laura spread her fingers across the screen and made it bigger. "How about now?"

"Eh? What?" The Engineer blinked quickly. "That's a copy of my design! Where did you—oh. *Oh*, I see. Now that's blood, isn't it?"

"Yeah." Laura sighed. "Like I said, the Gorafrex already took over two human hosts. Definitely woke up both their little peabrains, so there's that. And we have no idea who it jumped into after it...well, after it killed one witch already."

"This is the *witch's* blood?"

"Yes. On the wall. Apparently in the shape of your escape pod."

"Hmm. You must be very careful, Laura Hadstrom. This is old magic, yes? The Gorafrex is feeding on witches *and* using their magic to transmit power to the energy cores. By the looks of it, I'd say it already has one running."

Laura glanced at the picture of the large circle on her phone, twelve smaller circles drawn around it in blood like the face of a gruesome clock. The circle where a clock's number one would be was filled in with a white, opalescent substance. "Okay. So we go destroy that one—"

"That's a terrible idea. Unleashing that much lifeforce

magic will bring far too much attention to this. You need to dismantle as many of the energy cores as you can before that creature gets to them."

Turning off her phone, Laura stuffed it into her back pocket and gazed up at the Engineer. "How many?"

"All of them, preferably. That's impossible now. But as many as you can as quickly as you can, Laura Hadstrom. The ship *can* perform basic functions with only half of the energy cores online."

"So…seven. We need to destroy at least seven of them."

"As *many* as you can." Rutilda straightened on the stack of crates, her head rising tall above the young witch and casting her imposing shadow over her visitor. "Each time the Gorafrex fills another core, it will be more difficult for you to find and destroy the others."

Laura shook her head. "Why?"

"Blood magic powering a ship built millennia ago, now being awakened for the very first time? The havoc that would wreak on this larger ship's systems…on magic itself…" The Engineer dipped her head. "Well, it could do anything, really."

Yeah, that's incredibly helpful. Why can't we ever just get cut-and-dried warnings that say exactly what to expect? The young witch smiled grimly at the ancient giant living so far underground. "I guess we better start destroying energy cores. Is there a…way to go about doing that?"

"Ah. Yes, a good smashing should do the trick." The woman pounded one huge fist into her other hand.

"*Oh.* Okay. That's easy enough."

"Any way you can, Laura Hadstrom. By whatever

means necessary. Mostly, you must disconnect the conduction valves from the operations drive and—"

"I'm sorry." Laura spread her arms. "I have no idea what any of that means."

Rutilda chuckled. "No, I supposed not. Disconnect it, if you can. Destructive magic and physical force combined will give you the best odds. A good smashing, yes?"

"Right. Well…" Laura turned away from the woman and took a few steps across the platform toward the long catwalk. "I should get going. There's a lot to tell my sisters, and there's not a lotta time to lose, is there?"

"Yes. In this, I think, it's good that you are a hasty witch. Wait." The woman heaved herself to her feet, sending the remaining dust-covered tarps slipping to the cement platform, and shuffled toward another incomprehensible pile of junk. She bent down with a groan to rifle through the mess there, tossing whatever she didn't want behind her with no concern for her guest. Laura dodged a wad of coiled cables and a giant boot the size of a laundry basket before Rutilda finally stood upright. "This! Take this with you." The woman turned and took one huge step toward the young witch. "Useful for building *and* smashing."

Laura reached out with both hands to accept the huge, two-foot-long socket wrench. When the giant woman dropped it into her hand, Laura almost dropped it too. She grunted and clenched her fingers around the cold, worn metal. "Um…any special use for this?"

"Just do what feels right. It's never steered me wrong."

"Okay." Laura chuckled, then looked up to meet the Velikan Engineer's huge, round eyes. "Thank you, Rutilda. For the story and your knowledge of the…the *ship*." *Better not call it an escape pod again. Just in case I need to come back down here for another chat.* "And for this." She lifted the socket wrench in both hands and smiled.

"Just use what you can to do what you must, Laura Hadstrom." The giant woman bowed her head. "And if you manage to succeed relatively quickly, come back down to tell me all about it. Who knows how much longer I'll be here."

"I will. Promise." With another nod, the young witch turned away from the Velikan and made her way toward the long catwalk stretching across the gaping chasm. *Now I just gotta figure out how to carry this thing up the ladder...*

CHAPTER FOUR

E mily Hadstrom pulled the baking tin from the oven and grinned. "Oh, yeah. *This* is the best quiche I've ever made."

Nickie smirked at her little sister from the small kitchen table while warming her hands on a mug of fresh coffee. "You say that about everything you make."

Emily took a deep sniff of perfectly set eggs and tender asparagus, creamy brie and perfectly buttery, flaky crust, and sighed. "That's totally untrue. Remember those waffles?"

"The accidentally minty waffles?"

Emily shot her sister a warning glance. "That's my point. *Not* the best waffles I've ever made."

"Well *I* liked 'em."

"That literally means nothing, Nickie."

"Hey! What's that supposed to mean?"

Emily pulled three plates from the cabinet, then opened her knife drawer and found the serving knife exactly where she'd put it. *I'm so glad nobody else in this house cooks and messes with my stuff.* "It *means* that you have the least discerning palate of anyone I've ever met."

Nickie snorted. "What?"

"Come on." Emily leaned back against the counter. "You're twenty-four, and you still eat Pop-Tarts."

"I don't see anything wrong with that."

"Like I said. Least discerning palate. And that's why *I'm* the chef." Emily turned back toward the quiche to start slicing it.

"Not yet," Nickie muttered.

The youngest Hadstrom sister lifted her serving knife without turning around. "I heard that."

The stairs creaked with descending footsteps, and Laura rounded the corner from the dining room into the kitchen. "Smells amazing, Em."

"It's gonna taste even better." Emily served a sixth of the quiche onto each of their plates and popped a stray piece of asparagus into her mouth.

"Whoa." Nickie stared at their older sister shuffling into the kitchen. "Late night?"

Laura yawned and ran her fingers through her mess of uncombed hair. "Why?"

"If you sleep *any* less than seven hours, you get those bags under your eyes." Nickie gestured to her own eyes and grimaced.

Her older sister just blinked at her. "Any coffee left?"

"Should be."

Laura shuffled toward the coffee pot on the counter, and Emily brought all three plates and forks to the kitchen table. "Why were you up so late?" she asked before slipping into a chair.

"Coffee first."

They waited for Laura to complete her slower-than-usual process of pouring coffee, grabbing cream and sugar, and loading it into her cup. They'd learned getting between their oldest sister and her morning brew when she said 'coffee first' meant a bad day for all three of them. Laura took a long, slow sip, closed her eyes, and sighed; then, she took a seat in front of her plate of quiche.

"So?" Emily popped a forkful into her mouth and let out a moan of approval. "Go ahead and spill it."

"I *definitely* didn't get enough sleep last night." Laura cut up her breakfast, lifted her fork to her mouth, and paused. "I went out, actually."

"Huh," Nickie said through a mouthful. "I didn't hear you leave."

"I didn't hear you come back," Emily added.

"Hey, I can be quiet." Laura's sisters both snorted. "When I have to be."

"Sure, but you're never *thinking* about having to be quiet." Nickie twirled her fork beside her temple. "Whatever else you're thinking about at any given moment doesn't leave room for *being quiet*."

Laura rolled her eyes and kept eating.

And now she's too *quiet.* "Okay." Emily dropped her fork onto the plate with a clatter, and both her sisters glanced up at her in surprise. "You haven't said anything about the quiche, Laura."

"Oh. Oh, yeah. It's really good, Em. Thanks." Laura shoveled another bite into her mouth.

"I wasn't fishing for compliments." Emily stared at her sister and cocked her head. "But thanks. So how 'bout you tell us what you're thinking about so hard right now that you didn't say anything about my awesome quiche?"

Laura paused, took another bite, and washed it down with coffee.

"Hey, good call, Em." Nickie nodded slowly and studied her big sister. "We caught you, Laura. Now's the time to fess up."

"I was thinking about the best way to tell you guys what I did last night." Laura frowned into her coffee. "And *then* I was gonna tell you. As soon as I figured it out."

"There's nothing to figure out." Emily picked her fork up and continued eating. "Just say it."

"Oh, my god. Did you go out *with* someone?" Nickie grinned.

"Ha!" Emily pointed her fork at the oldest Hadstrom sister. "You went on a *date!*"

"*What?* I did *not* go on a—no. Just no." Laura shook her head.

"Then what is it? That's a slice of the best quiche I've ever made, and you're not even *tasting* it!"

"Okay, cut it out about the quiche, Emily." Laura sat back in her chair and gazed with exhausted eyes at her sisters. "Fine. I'll just put it out there."

"Please do."

"Em…" Nickie shook her head.

"Remember that map Dad drew for us after we told him about…well, our little Gorafrex problem?"

"The map to where the Engineer lives, yeah." Nickie folded her arms.

"Yeah, well, I can tell you guys right now Dad sucks at

drawing maps." Laura blinked in surprise, like she hadn't meant to say that at all.

Emily gasped. "You didn't..." Her sister wouldn't meet her gaze, and she slapped her hands down on the table. "You *did*. Come on, Laura."

"Wait, you went to look for the Engineer without us?" Nickie frowned, and Laura dipped her head, staring at her half-eaten slice of quiche.

"I thought we kinda made it clear when we *made a plan* that *this* wasn't a solo Laura adventure." Emily scoffed. "I switched my *shifts* so we'd all have the same night off. I don't switch my shifts, Laura. Not at—"

"Not at Meadowlark Tavern. I know." Laura nodded.

"So why'd you ditch us?" Nickie asked.

"I didn't *ditch* you guys."

"Yeah. You did." Emily mimed a little toss. "Like a bad habit."

"Okay, fine. I went by myself because I thought that was the best chance of getting the information we needed."

"That doesn't make *any* sense."

"Oh, come on. You guys know you don't always make the best first impression. Nickie just floats around, going with the flow. Totally distracted. I mean, you were dancing around *barefoot* when we went to find the Tree Folk."

"What does that have to do with anything?" Nickie blinked. "You know, I also played the music that brought them out to talk to us in the first place."

"Yeah, but this was an *Engineer*. One of the original Velikan who designed and built this whole ship. That's like a meeting with the President of UT or the CEO of Google."

Emily scratched her head. "Not really."

"See? That's what I mean." Laura pointed at her youngest sister. "You always have some last-minute jab to get in or…just really awful jokes." She cocked her head and blinked at her coffee mug. "Actually, Rutilda probably would've really liked you…"

"Who's Rutilda?"

Laura glanced up at Emily and shrugged. "The Engineer. Honestly, I think she's startin' to lose it. Makes sense, really. Being down there by herself for who knows how—"

"Woah, woah, woah, wait." Emily lifted a hand to stop her sister's rambling. "Back up. You *found* the Engineer?"

"Yeah."

"And you talked to her?"

"Yeah, that's what I've been saying this whole time…" Laura frowned at them. "I didn't say that, did I?"

Nickie raised her eyebrows. "Nope."

"So now would be the right time to tell us what she told you." Emily jammed another forkful of quiche into her mouth.

"Okay." Laura sighed. "I showed her that symbol the Gorafrex left on the wall at that woman's house. She knew exactly what it was…because she designed it."

When Laura finished telling her sisters everything Rutilda had said, the kitchen fell quiet.

"So…" Emily frowned. "We thought we had to keep that thing from possessing any more humans and killing other witches or wizards. And now we're switching gears to finding and bashing up the energy cores of an escape pod so the Gorafrex doesn't destroy the planet, er, ship. Does that cover everything?"

"Pretty much. Yeah." Laura raised her eyebrows and shrugged. "I mean, if we end up finding the Gorafrex first and putting it back in its prison, we should definitely do that."

"But we haven't even figured out *how*," Nickie said. "Sure, we know Dad's lullaby calls it like a giant homing beacon. And that I almost played myself into a coma trying to get it into Tina's laundromat. But it didn't work."

"It almost worked." Laura pointed at her.

"And then the Gorafrex found an unsuspecting witch in the parking lot and completely ignored us so it could kidnap her…and then murder her." Nickie shook her head. "If I'm gonna play that song again to capture it, I need to figure out how to use Dad's ring to keep me from being useless afterward." She glanced at the black Hadstrom legacy ring on her thumb—the same ring their Dad had worn as a protector of the Gorafrex prison before that responsibility fell to his daughters. "I can't just pass out and let you guys fight it by yourselves."

"Yeah, and I'd *really* like to figure out how those weird yo-yo things are supposed to be weapons." Emily cocked her head at Laura. "You sure you have no idea what they're for? You did make them."

Laura shook her head. "I'm pretty sure the ring made them. I just let it use my magic. I think."

Biting her lip, Emily turned to Nickie. "Hear any more drums?"

"Not since the night that thing got away from us."

"Well, at least we know the Gorafrex isn't trying to lure

in another witch or wizard with the creepy drumbeats." Laura smoothed her dark hair—the same color all three sisters had inherited—away from her face. "For now. Until you hear the drums again, Nickie, we have time to find the energy cores."

"The Engineer didn't happen to tell you where to find them, did she?" Emily leaned back in her chair and raised her eyebrows.

"No..." Laura grinned. "But we have a map."

"Huh?"

"The symbol on the wall, Em."

"*Oh*. Right. We just gotta walk in a big giant circle around Austin and start bashing up energy cores?"

Laura closed her eyes and tried not to snap at her sister. "I'm pretty sure it's a little more complicated than that. Rutilda said the prison in the Greenbelt is at the center of the smaller ship."

"And where are the energy cores?" Nickie asked.

"My guess is the first one was somewhere around that woman's house."

"The house where a witch was murdered by the possessed human whose tiny magical peabrain woke up three days ago?"

"Yeah, Em. That house."

Emily glanced from Laura to Nickie and pursed her lips. "Anybody hear anything about either of the humans the Gorafrex woke up to their own magic?"

"Nope." Nickie shrugged. "But they have to figure out how to handle magic on their own now that they know they have it. They'll be fine."

"Yeah..." Emily sighed and dug into the quiche crust

with her fork. "I can't help feeling a little bad for them, though. It's gotta be pretty hard waking up one day after being possessed by a bodiless witch-murderer and finding out you have all this magic with no idea how to use it or what it's for or what you're gonna do next."

Nickie chuckled. "Do you feel sorry for us too?"

"What?"

Laura smirked. "You basically just described us, Em. I mean, without the being-possessed-by-a-Gorafrex part."

"Oh." Emily snorted. "Guess we're all just trying to figure things out as we go along, huh?"

"Sometimes, that's all we got."

CHAPTER FIVE

After helping her sisters clean up breakfast—and making sure to tell Emily one more time how good the quiche was, because it *was* delicious—Laura headed up the stairs of their magically enhanced house on Pressler Street and went to her room. She'd been walking up the same stairs and taking the same right turn on the second-floor landing for years, but three days wasn't nearly enough time to break the last part of that long-time habit.

She stopped in front of her bedroom door and reached toward her back pocket for her wand, which wasn't there. "Right. Not carrying it around anymore. Because *you*"—she glanced at the silver ring on her thumb—"seem to be doing all the work now, don't you?" Raising her palm toward the door, she only had to think about checking the wards she'd put up around her room—which she'd also started doing since the Gorafrex *killed* a witch who never saw it coming. Her ring flashed silver. The wards shimmered to life with an orange glow in front of her. "No such thing as being too careful." The wards rippled as she grasped the doorknob, opened the door, and stepped inside.

Sunlight spilled through the curtain over her window, lighting up her L-shaped desk in the far right corner and her bed just beside the door, which she'd made even before getting coffee. "Okay. Now the coffee's kicking in." Laura rubbed her hands together. "Let's make a map."

Years ago, before she'd reached her current status as the University of Texas' youngest tenured archaeology professor, Laura figured out how to combine a few spells to take her own crash course in amateur cartography. "This might just be the most useful thing I've ever done with it." She lifted her hand toward the middle of her room and muttered, "*Ostende* Austin."

Glittering purple lines appeared in the air, scrolling longer and reaching out from the center until a detailed map of the city hovered in front of her. Laura smirked. "Maybe I should send in a patent for this. Like Google Maps for witches." She stepped closer to the purple lines and studied the map. "Okay. The woman's house was down here in McKinney Park East…" Her silver ring flashed, and a glowing yellow dot appeared on the street where the magical Tibetan singing bowl she'd bought from Carl Hopkins—which also doubled as a magical-frequency tracker—had led her and her sisters three days ago. "Only we just didn't get there fast enough, did we? We will this time. No more dead witches or wizards."

Studying the map, Laura pointed at the Barton Creek Greenbelt running through the center of Austin. "And that's the center of the prison. So…" She drew a white circle around the map, starting from the woman's house, up, and around, keeping the Greenbelt in the center. Then she intersected it with six lines and had her twelve equally spaced points plotted and done. "So these are our energy cores." The silver ring glowed each time she tapped the places where the white lines met the white circle. Eleven yellow dots glowed in her spell, and she stepped back to take it all in.

"Great. So we've got another neighborhood. More neighborhoods…" She traced the circle with her eyes, west and north and around. "Okay, a few public parks. Not so bad—wait." The impulse to spread her fingers along the map was almost too hard to ignore. "Well, hey. If the Engineers did their job with magic *and* technology, so can I."

Stepping toward her bedside table, Laura snatched up her phone and pulled up a map of Austin on the internet. She zoomed in to where she'd placed a dot for an energy core right off I-35. "You've gotta be kidding me." She double-checked her purple map in the air, then looked at her phone again. "There's an energy core at the Thinkery? They just *had* to build a children's museum on top of an escape pod energy core, didn't they? Perfect. That's literally the worst place to—" The location of the last dot on her map made her groan. "Okay, two of the worst places. A children's museum and the airport." Biting her lip, Laura took a deep breath and let herself settle into what she and her sisters would have to do next. "This is gonna be interesting."

"Hey, you guys?" Laura turned right off the stairs in the foyer and stepped into the spacious living room. "I think I found the energy cores we should look for first…" She stopped when she found Nickie sprawled out on the couch, reading what looked like a horror novel from an author Laura had never heard of. Their immortal bulldog Speed stretched himself out across Nickie's bare feet, snoring away even this early in the morning. *Probably getting ready to clear the room any minute, too.* The dog's nauseating gas problem made her hold her breath for a second until she was certain the air was clear. "Where's Emily?"

"Work." Nickie lowered the book and looked up. "She said that right before you went upstairs."

"Oh…right. I can just Sister Soup her again—"

"Laura, I really wouldn't."

"Why not?"

Nickie raised her eyebrows. "She was kinda pissed the last time your face showed up in the actual soup she was making."

"She told you about that?"

"Yeah." Chuckling, Nickie set the book aside and pushed up to sit sideways against the couch's back cushion. Speed didn't stir on top of her feet. "I mean, we have cell phones for a reason."

"But that was an emergency. Emily doesn't answer her phone at work, so Sister Soup was the only way I could get hold of her."

"Is this an emergency too?"

Laura opened her mouth, paused, and puffed out a breath. "Not right now. No…"

"So text her. She'll see it on her break."

"I honestly don't think she *takes* breaks."

Nickie smirked. "Yeah, probably not. She'll see it when she's off, though. I think she said she's off at three."

"I just don't want her to make any plans."

"On a Friday night, Laura? Good luck."

"Really?" Laura folded her arms. "I think keeping the Gorafrex from killing someone else to turn on another energy core is a *little* more important than Emily's social life."

"Hey, I'm totally with you there. But I don't have the night off, either." Laura's confusion must have been too obvious, because Nickie cocked her head in disappointment. "Come on…I have a show tonight. Which I also told you about. That's why we *were* gonna go look for the Engineer tomorrow night. All of us. Together."

"Right. Tomorrow. Okay." Laura licked her lips and glanced around the living room. "I just think we should get a head start on this. Maybe I should go to Thinkery by myself, since you guys are busy. Check the place out, see if there's—"

"Woah. Slow down." Nickie draped her arm over the back of the couch. "Going off by yourself to talk to that Engineer is one thing, but it's a really bad idea to go looking for an energy core without us. We don't know where the Gorafrex is, or which energy core it's going for next, or even *how to stop it*—wait. Did you say the Thinkery?"

"Yeah." Laura plopped down in an old, super comfy armchair across from the couch. "I plotted the map for all twelve energy cores. Most of them are neighborhoods or parks. One's right in the Colorado River. And then there's the children's museum."

"Jeeze…"

"And the airport."

Nickie blinked. "You're kidding."

"No."

"Oh, boy. Yeah. Text Emily. We should go tomorrow for sure. God, just the thought of that thing around a bunch of kids…"

"I know." Laura swallowed, then pulled her phone out and started a text to their youngest sister. "Here's hoping tomorrow's not too late."

"We'll be fine." Nickie lay down, propping her head up on the pillow against the armrest. "I haven't heard the drums in a few days. Trust me, I'd be hearing that pounding in my head even if the Gorafrex was all the way out in Brenham."

Laura snorted. "Well if the drums come back, you'll tell me, right?"

"Of course. It's not like I can hide a massive migraine like that, anyway." Nickie picked up her book and opened it to the dog-eared page.

How is she so laid-back about all this is? And why *does she keep folding those page corners?* It took a lot of willpower not to ask either of those questions, so she focused on finishing her text and sent it. "What are you doing the rest of the day?"

Nickie shrugged even as she kept reading. "Chuck wants to have lunch. I might practice for a little after that, then we'll head over to Gruene Hall."

"Oh, my god. I totally forgot. *That's* your show tonight."

Peering at Laura over the top of her book, Nickie wiggled her eyebrows. "*That's* my show. I got you a ticket, so you should come. It's gonna be a blast. Might be good for you. Forget about work or the Gorafrex or energy cores for a while."

"I'll be there." *Doesn't mean I can't spend my time* before *the show thinking about energy cores...*

CHAPTER SIX

E mily had been in a kitchen in some way or another since she was old enough to work. Granted, she'd been sixteen, and that first job had been as a dishwasher at Applebee's. Even then, she'd only taken breaks when the manager pulled her aside and told her she legally had to make Emily sit down or leave the kitchen for at least ten minutes.

Since she'd gotten the commis chef gig at Meadowlark Tavern, though, she couldn't remember the last time she'd had a break. There weren't any managers around to make sure their minimum-wage employees followed Texas State law. Emily ran with the big dogs now—almost—and the chefs at Meadowlark took their breaks at their own peril. Chef Ansler told her when he'd hired her, "If you think you can slip out for five, maybe ten minutes without anyone noticing, go for it. But if you neglect your station and anything on the line slows down 'cause you're not there, you're done."

Naturally, Emily never left her station. *I can take breaks when I have my own restaurant. 'Til then, it's head down and get to work. I can do this.* She took the giant plastic container of mushroom soup on tonight's menu into the walk-in, and the second she stepped back out, Chef Ansler shouted, "Hadstrom!"

"Yes, Chef."

"How's the mushroom bisque coming?"

"Just put it away, Chef."

"Good. Go take a break."

Emily paused on her way back to her station and stared at the Head Chef of Meadowlark Tavern. He mentioned something to Chef Alyssa, the sauté chef, then met Emily's gaze.

"Ten minutes, Hadstrom." He jerked his thumb toward the back door. "I don't wanna see you in my kitchen 'til they're up."

"Yes, Chef." She unbuttoned her chef's coat and hung it in the staff room just off the kitchen, then she grabbed her cell phone from her locker and headed out the back door. *Either he's getting ready to sack me for something I have no clue I did...or he's likes what I'm doing enough to make me take a break.* With a snort, she went and sat on the median curb on the other side of the back lot beneath two dogwoods. "Jeeze. Eleven o'clock and this hot already." She unlocked her phone and pulled up a text from Laura.

'Found the other energy cores. There's one at Thinkery. We're going tomorrow.'

Emily gawked at her phone. "Are you freakin' *kidding* me?"

"Bad news?"

She jerked her head up. John stood in front of her in the

shade.

Emily grinned. "More like my sister being a serious downer."

"Which one? Wait. Lemme guess." He pointed at her. "Laura."

"Okay, well when I described my sisters to you as Austin's new Queen of Blues and *the serious archaeologist,* it's pretty much a no-brainer which one." She puffed out a chuckle. "I should also add that Laura *can* be fun when she loosens up. She's not all business all the time. Just most of the time. And hi."

"Hi." John smiled, then that smile went to a baffled frown. "Wait. You didn't describe her as the new Queen of Blues. You said Nickie was a blues rock musician."

"She is." Emily laughed and stood from the curb. "Most people put two and two together."

"Your last name's Hadstrom?"

"Yep."

"And Nickie Hadstrom is your *sister?*"

"Okay, time to pick your jaw off the floor."

John grabbed his hair with both hands and laughed in disbelief. "Holy crap. That's amazing! Is she as badass in real as she is onstage?"

"Mm...sometimes." Emily shrugged and couldn't hide another smile. "Most of the time, she's just...out there. I mean, she's definitely cool. She just kinda does her own thing. Little bit of spacey, little bit of weird thrown in. Honestly, Nickie's pretty much a female version of our dad." She choked back another laugh.

"Oh, my god. Because your *dad's* Greg Hadstrom, right?"

"Yeah, that's what happens with siblings."

John laughed. "Sorry. I've never met a famous person before."

"It's okay." Emily leaned toward him and whispered. "You still haven't."

"Ha, ha. Very funny." He threw his arms up, then shot her a sideways glance. "You think I could meet her?"

"She's got a boyfriend, John."

"What? No, not like—" He chuckled and ran a hand through his hair. With a nervous lick of his lips, he glanced at Emily and sighed. "That's not what I meant."

"Just a fan, then, huh?"

He spread his arms. "Purely fan-style."

Emily smirked. "What are you doing tonight?"

"Uh…" John glanced at Meadowlark Tavern's back door. "Working."

"Well, yeah. But when do you get off?"

"Probably seven. Maybe seven-thirty."

"Okay." Emily took a deep breath and headed toward the door. "You'll probably miss the opener, unless you get cut early. But I'm pretty sure I can get you in."

"What, *tonight*?" He stopped in the middle of the lot and stared at her.

When she turned around and saw his wide, dumbstruck eyes, she laughed. "Yeah. Tonight. Gruene Hall."

"I think you just became my favorite person." He hurried to catch up with her.

"Besides Nickie Hadstrom, right?" Emily pulled the back door open, stepped through, and held it open for him until he pushed against it himself and walked inside behind her.

"Yeah, but I don't know her. I know *you*." They turned the corner into the staff room. "I like knowing you."

"John, are you flirting with me or just brown-nosing 'cause I said I could get you into the show tonight?"

He paused at his locker, blinked, and turned to her with a shrug. "Both?" Her laugh made him grin. "Yeah, I'm gonna go with both."

"Well, okay." Emily grabbed her chef's coat from the hook and slipped it on. "I know we're about to open for lunch, and you'll probably still be busy by the time I get outta here. So…" She nodded toward the staff list tacked to the wall. "My number's up there. Lemme know when you're on your way."

He grinned. "Totally."

"Cool." She headed out of the staff room.

"Hey, Emily."

She looked at him over her shoulder. "Yeah?"

"Is this a date?"

"Only if you don't go crazy-fanboy and ignore me the whole time."

"Fair enough."

Grinning, she turned around and went to her station. *Okay, that was totally unplanned. And it's not technically a rebound if I wasn't really that upset about breaking up with Jeremy less than two weeks ago, right?* She shrugged and stopped in front of her station as a sous chef, at least for now. *Laura's totally gonna have something to say about that too.*

Beside her at the potager station, Chef Martino jerked his chin up and shot her a sideways glance. "What are you so slap-happy about?"

Emily wrinkled her nose and shook her head. "I'm not

slap-happy." She couldn't help glancing back at the staff room, though, as John headed through the kitchen with his server's apron tied around his waist. He turned to walk backward a few steps and throw horns at her with both hands. She snorted and shook her head, but the grin didn't go away.

"Oh, *I* get it." Chef Martino chuckled as he chopped some green onions. "Whatever it is, don't let Chef Ansler see it."

Emily frowned at her former mentor. "It's none of his business."

"Everything in this kitchen is his business. He'll make things hell for both of you, so I'd act like you don't even know the guy's name."

"That's ridiculous."

Chef Martino shrugged. "My advice. Your call."

"Okay, well, thank you very much." Emily rolled her eyes, and the man chuckled without looking up. She grabbed another huge plastic storage container and got to work on the second soup option. *I've never let a guy get between me and a kitchen. If Jeremy couldn't change my mind, John definitely won't. Okay, focus, Em. Remember what happened last time you let your wishful thinking run wild on the line?*

She glanced at the copper legacy ring on her thumb; fortunately, there was no flash of magic. She still hadn't learned how to use it instead of her wand. Still, even while she grabbed a tomato and her Shun chef's knife, she couldn't wipe the smile off her face.

Maybe I should start taking more breaks.

CHAPTER SEVEN

Nickie sipped her beer on Cedar Door's crowded back patio. The weather app on her phone showed Austin had already reached the standard hundred-and-one degrees of a classic summer day. Despite the misters blowing clouds of cool water over everyone on the patio, sweat dripped down her forehead. *We should've just gotten takeout and gone to his place. At least he has AC. And my house just has magic...*

"Hey, babe." Chuck peered around her shoulder and grinned.

"Finally."

He gave her a quick kiss, then slipped onto the stool beside her at the bar. "Sorry I'm late. Dave just kept..." He mimed a yacking mouth with his hand and rolled his eyes. "Like he still doesn't get it that this was technically a business meeting and not me coming over to hang out and shoot the shit."

Nickie chuckled. "That meeting was today, huh?"

"Yeah. I told you that last night." A small frown creased

his brow, then Chuck pulled his shirt away from his chest and shook it. "*Man*. You know, it'd be really nice if being a native made you a *little* immune to the heat. Right? Like I think we deserve that. We're still here. By choice." He spread his arms and threw his head back at the sky—with the patio ceiling between them. "How 'bout a little break?"

"If you can wait it out long enough for a beer, I think you'll be okay." Her boyfriend-turned-manager lowered his head to shoot her an amused glance, and Nickie winked. "Next time, though, maybe we eat in when it's this hot out."

"Yeah, but I didn't wanna make you drive all the way across town just for lunch…"

"I drive *all the way across town* just to sit on your couch and binge-watch Netflix." Nickie raised an eyebrow. "And it's only, like, fifteen minutes."

Chuck snorted shook his head. "Okay, you win. Next time, I'll make you drive to me."

"Oh, you'll *make* me, huh?"

"Well, yeah. If going out for lunch is off the table and you still wanna see *this* gorgeous face…"

Nickie barked out a laugh, grabbed his face with both hands and pulled him in for a long kiss. It wasn't as long as she wanted, though. Another laugh escaped her, and she had to pull away to wipe her mouth and nose with the back of her hand. "You are *so* sweaty."

Chuck wiggled his eyebrows. "So are you."

The bartender slid toward them behind the bar and nodded. "What can I getcha?"

"That, please." Chuck pointed at Nickie's beer. "And we're eating, too."

"Yup." The bartender slid another menu and rolled

silverware in front of Chuck, then set down a cold beer with the lid popped off in about three seconds.

"Thank you—and… he's already gone." Chuck raised his beer at the bartender's back, then lifted it again toward Nickie. "To sweaty lunches before a sweaty show." She laughed and tapped her beer against his. "You're still gonna do that, right?"

Nickie shot him a playful frown. "Duh. I *did* check the weather for tonight, actually. Down to seventy-two, I think, by the time I go on. So yeah, I'll dress accordingly."

"You always do." They took long pulls of their beers, and Chuck sighed. "Okay. So. Wanna hear the news?"

She raised her eyebrows. "About what?"

"About what? Babe. I just came from Dave's…"

"Oh. Right." She nodded. "Right. Sorry. Yeah, I totally wanna hear all about it."

He set his beer down on the bar, propped one elbow up on it, too, and spun his stool to face her head-on. "Nickie, are you okay?"

"What?" Her smile widened, but it felt a little forced. "Of course I'm okay. Why wouldn't I be?"

"I have absolutely no idea. Which is why I'm asking." Chuck studied her face, and the tiny frown of concern reappeared. "You've just been a little off the last couple days." Nickie glanced down at her hand around the beer bottle resting on her thigh. "Like just a little more…spacey than normal. And don't get me wrong." He dipped his head toward her to grab her attention, and Nickie's gaze flickered up to meet his. "I love spacey Nickie Hadstrom. Like, more than anything." She pressed her lips together through her smirk. "But it seems like there's something else going on."

"I don't know…" Nickie took a deep breath and sighed.

"Are you nervous about the show?"

"What?"

Chuck shrugged. "I mean, it's been a while since you played there, and you had a lot less going on the last time. If you're nervous, I totally get it."

"Yeah, maybe that's it." Nickie tipped her beer back for a few swigs.

And now I have to lie to him again. Can't tell my human boyfriend that Laura unleashed a witch-killing monster and now we have to go shut down the escape pod it's apparently trying to power up again. 'Cause that would mean telling him I'm a witch.

She put her beer down and realized she'd downed all of it.

Blinking, Chuck nodded at the empty bottle. "Sure looks like it."

She snorted. "You caught me." *Okay, might as well tie a little bit of truth to the lie.* "I don't know, babe. Things have just been a little weird lately. And Laura's got this… project she's working on. I think it's for one of her classes, but she wants me and Emily to come with her tomorrow to look for some *antique* somewhere or something."

"Again?" Chuck raised an eyebrow. "I mean, I get that she's super into her work, but so are you. And yeah, I know. If you have the time to go with her, you will, because that's the kinda person you are. One of the perks of not having to work a nine-to-five. I'm right there with you." He grabbed her hand on the bar and gave it a little squeeze.

"But if doing Laura a favor is messing with you like this, it's okay to tell her no sometimes."

"I know that." She squeezed his fingers in reply. "But… well, she's my sister."

"Yeah. You know, I think the only time I've ever wished I wasn't an only child is when you and your sisters say it like that. Like it just…explains why you make certain decisions."

"It kinda does." *Doesn't explain why I'm using her as a scapegoat right now. That's not super awesome.*

"Hey, what if I came with you guys tomorrow? Hopefully, I still make things a little more fun when I'm around." He chuckled.

"Oh…no, Chuck. You don't have to do that—"

"I totally will. I have no problem being in antique stores or wherever you're going. And your sisters love me. I think."

Nickie laughed and shook her head. "They do. It's just… I think maybe Laura planned the whole thing for just the three of us? And she's been *really* picky about how things get done. Like yesterday, she ripped me a new one because I hung up one of her shirts on the wrong-colored hanger."

"Woah. I mean, I know she's super organized, but that's intense."

"It wasn't about the hanger, though. Not really." Nickie shook her head, half at Laura's quirks and half at herself for how much deeper she was digging this hole. *At least the hanger part's true.* "When she gets focused on something or has some problem to work out, she tends to blow everything else outta proportion." She shrugged with an almost-playful grimace.

"Huh. So you think me being there would set her off?"

Oh, thank god that worked. "Yeah. Sorry, babe. *But* she said she's coming to the show tonight. You could ask her. See if she's open to it." *And she would definitely tell him no.*

"No, that's okay." Chuck smiled and scratched the back of his blond head. "You know, I think I've only seen her freak out once or twice, but it left enough of an impression for me to know better. And if she's coming to watch you tonight, I want us to be able to focus on how incredibly *magical* you are onstage." Despite the heat and both of them dripping with sweat, he cupped her cheek and leaned toward her. "Because you really are."

"Thank you." *He has no clue how literal that sentence was.*

He kissed her, then pulled away and laughed. "I know. Sorry. Super sweaty."

"Yeah." Nickie licked her lips this time and grinned. "I like it."

"*There* she is!" Chuck's bright-blue eyes sparkled when he smiled back at her. "You make that kinda weirdness *really* sexy, you know that?"

"Damn right I do." *Okay, no more lying. Let's move past it.* "Chuck, I promise I'm not taking any of this onstage with me. I'm goin' up there to play tonight."

"Hey, I know that. You're a pro." He winked at her and took a long drink of his beer before wiping his sweat-beaded forehead on his arm. "Whew."

"Okay." Nickie propped both elbows on the bar and wiggled her eyebrows. "So tell me how your meeting with Dave went."

"Oh, the *meeting*…" He eyed her sideways. "You know, I got kinda worried when you didn't ask right away."

"Yeah, well, now I'm asking." She slapped his arm with the back of her hand and laughed. "So *tell* me."

"Well, all his nonstop talking aside…"

"Chuck. Spit it out."

"Yeah, he wants to sign you."

"Yes!" Nickie pumped her fist, and only when she caught the closest dozen people at the restaurant turning to look at her did she realize how loud she'd shouted. She hunched her shoulders with a laugh and grinned. "*Yes*. He wants to sign me?"

"He wants to sign *you*, Nickie Hadstrom. Blue Silk Records and the new Queen of Blues are gonna *kill* it together."

"I'm about to have a freakin' record deal!" She let out a squeak, jumped off the stool, and flung her arms around his neck. Neither one of them noticed the heat or the sweat this time when she almost knocked him to the floor with another kiss that was longer and more intense. The bartender approached them twice before they stopped long enough for him to ask if they were ready to order lunch.

CHAPTER EIGHT

Laura hurried from the staff parking lot to the Liberal Arts building on the University of Texas campus. "Can't say I don't appreciate the perks of this job," she muttered, gazing over the mostly-empty campus. "No classes to teach this summer, and I can *still* be here whenever I want. Instant resources. I hope."

As soon as she reached the front door and pulled down on the handle, someone shouted behind her: "Excuse me. Wait! Please. Can you hold the door?"

Laura turned to see a pair of long legs in jeans sticking out from the bottom of a huge, perilous stack of boxes. Despite the fact that the owner of those legs had to be over six feet tall, the boxes in his arms blocked his face.

"Sure." Laura stepped aside and held the door while the man awkwardly tried to hurry. *Like me holding this door is a lot harder than carrying all that stuff...*

He sidled through the door, trying to give her enough personal space while also not losing any boxes. That plan failed when a corner of the second-to-highest box caught the doorframe and started to slide off.

Laura lifted her finger to point at the sliding package, and the silver legacy ring on her thumb flashed. A muffled thump came from the box as it shoved back into place on the stack, and the man stumbled the rest of the way inside.

She held her breath. *Oh, good one, Laura. Now you get to try explaining how you...what?*

The man stopped inside the door, leaning at a painful-looking angle to keep the boxes stacked in his arms. He studied Laura with a grin, his eyes dancing with amusement and a faint but telltale purple hue she hadn't seen in quite a while. "I appreciate the help."

"Don't worry about it." Laura tried to smile, but her lips only made it as far as a grimace, so she dropped it. *What in the world is a Kashgar doing at this school?*

The man turned sideways, trying to peer beyond his armful of boxes and down the hallways. "Um...mind pointing me toward A107?"

Laura let the door close behind her. "What do you need in A107?"

"Well..." He chuckled. "To put these boxes down, for starters."

"Oh. Right." Stepping past him, she pointed to the left hallway. "Down there." Then she turned down that same hallway and hurried off, ready to be away from him. *Just a little weird seeing a Kashgar delivery boy. Didn't think they took jobs like that, but whatever. He'll be in and out of here, and that's it.*

Most of the doors lining the hall were locked, their windows dark. She passed three that stayed open during the summer, but most of the sound came from ahead in the Archaeology Program's main office. "Perfect. Maybe I'll only have to ask my questions once."

She rounded the corner and found some colleagues inside the main office, gathered next to the department director's private office on the other side of the reception desk. Someone finished a joke, and all six of them—four senior instructors and two professors—broke into appreciative chuckles.

Rebecca Marlow, who taught Anthropology 101 two days a week, noticed Laura's arrival. "*Hi*, Laura." The woman grinned and raised a hand to wiggle her fingers. The others turned from their circle to face the newcomer.

"Rebecca." Laura succeeded in smiling this time. *I've been working here for two years, and she* still *talks to me like she did when I took her class.*

"How's your summer going?" A female instructor Laura didn't know studied her with an intense gaze and what looked like a little blush.

Guess I shouldn't be surprised people I don't know know who I am. That's what I get for breaking records here. Laura sighed. "Honestly, it's been a little hectic."

"I thought you weren't teaching any classes this summer?" Rebecca frowned.

That's false concern and *disappointment, right there.* "Oh, I'm not. Just figured I'd come in and get a head start on some of my research."

"You never stop, do you?"

"It's amazing," the other instructor whispered. Beside her, the middle-aged man in a tweed jacket—which wasn't as bad of an idea as it seemed when this building, at least, had working AC—chuckled and folded his arms.

"Um…thanks." She looked at the man in the tweed jacket. "Winston, I was wondering if I could borrow you for a few minutes. Pick your brain about a couple things."

Winston blinked and unfolded his arms. "Absolutely. You always ask the best questions."

Oh, good. Another jibe from a former professor turned coworker. And he even recommended me for this position…

Laura kept the mask of her smile fastened. "Thank you. The rest of you, have a great weekend."

A chorus of, "You too," and "Good to see you, Laura," followed her out of the main office. Smiling softly, Winston stepped out with her into the hall. "I have to say I'm flattered you want my opinion on anything," he said, his voice low and drawn-out.

Laura folded her arms and leaned against the wall. "Well, you've been around a while, right?"

The much older archaeology professor—who also happened to be an elf—tipped his head back and studied her from over the bridge of his nose. "A handful of centuries. Just barely reached my prime."

"Do you know anything about…prisons?"

He frowned. The bubble of magic that kept his appearance hidden from *un-awakened* humans didn't extend the same illusion to Laura—or any other magical who already understood who and what they were. Laura found herself wanting to push his left eyebrow down, which turned up away from his face at a much sharper angle than the right. "In what era?"

"In the—" She glanced behind her and shot a curt smile

at the student taking her own sweet time to walk past them and around the corner. "The *original* era." *I really hope he doesn't make me say it out loud here in the hallway.*

Winston blinked. "The original?"

She nodded with wide eyes.

"Laura, I don't believe the original design included prisons. Screened and approved passengers only."

"Right." Laura sighed. "Okay, forget about the prison part. I'm gonna switch gears." *And try not to completely give everything away.* "I have a lead on an...artifact. Only it's buried under a building that sees a lot of traffic."

The middle-aged elf narrowed his eyes and cocked his head. "This doesn't have anything to do with your research, does it?"

"No. Sorry. This is me coming to you as a..." She glanced around. "...*magical person* who needs some advice from a fellow magical person with a lot more wisdom."

Please, Winston. Take the compliment and help me.

"I see. Well a handful of centuries has certainly given me *that*..."

"Good. So, this is sort of a time-sensitive thing, here. Do you have any suggestions for how to *get* to this artifact without drawing any attention? Or how to find out where it is?"

"You don't know the exact location?"

Laura shook her head. "Just the building."

"Any other objects connected to this artifact? Something you can draw from to use as a tracer?"

She put a hand on her hip. "Winston, if I had something like that, I wouldn't be asking for help."

His long eyebrows drew up, quivering at the ends.

"Right. Then, no, Laura. I can't help you find an exact location without any other connection to the artifact. As to getting inside, I'd suggest a transport bubble."

"Really?"

Winston shrugged. "Peabrain magic is very direct. Gets right to the point, despite such small numbers of those using it."

"Okay…" Laura blinked. *Good to know the magic I've studied the least is going to be the most helpful right now.* "I definitely hadn't considered that, so thank you."

"I hope it helps. Oh, you might consider talking to Phyllis about how to pinpoint a location without any real anchor, so to speak."

"Phyllis? How does a specialization in the modern repercussions of…*oh.*"

Winston smiled and dipped his head. "It's a shot in the dark, but something tells me that's more than what you have right now."

Cute. "Okay. Well, thanks for your time, Winston. The bubble suggestion was helpful."

"Anytime." The elf gave her a half bow, then lifted a finger. "You know, I heard the other day that we have a Kashgar joining us for the fall semester. Not sure when he's coming into town, but seeing as he's—"

"A Mechanic. I know. I'll keep it in mind. Thanks again." Laura turned and headed down the hallway before rounding the corner. "I am *not* going to Phyllis for help." She pulled her keys out of her back pocket, her hiking boots echoing on the linoleum floors. "I swear that fae tried to sabotage my dissertation. Can't prove it, but I saw her smug grin when I couldn't find the slides…" With a grunt of frustration, she shook her head and stopped outside her office door, room A110. "And who in their right mind would hire a—"

"Well, look at that."

Laura whirled and peered across the hall and a few doors down. The man with the giant stack of boxes stood in the open doorway of A107. *The Kashgar. Oh, no…* Unable to change how wide her eyes were, she settled for pursing her lips. "What are *we* looking at?"

He chuckled. "Sorry. I just…honestly, I thought you were a student."

Yeah, I hear that a lot. Laura blinked at him. "Well, I thought you were a delivery man, so…" She shrugged and turned toward her office. She got as far as slipping the key into the lock before he made it clear he wasn't giving up.

"I'm actually teaching this fall."

"Yes, I see that." She unlocked her door and pushed it open. *The last thing I need right now is some Kashgar sniffing around and making more trouble for me. 'Cause that's what they do.*

She flipped on the light switch, stepped in and went to her desk. The key in her top-right drawer unlocked the bottom-right drawer, which was what she intended to do when she sat in her swiveling desk chair.

"What do you teach?"

She slammed the top drawer closed, pinching the tip of her finger in the process. Sucking in a breath, she shook out her hand and eyed the Kashgar standing in *her* doorway. *What does he* want?"

"Archaeology," she muttered. *Wow, that sounded rude.*

Tone it down a little. Attempting a smile, she asked, "What about you?"

"Advanced Physics."

"This is the Liberal Arts building."

"I know. I think this was the closest empty office, so here I am."

"Great." Laura blinked, smiled, and returned to her desk drawer.

"I'm Nathan." The man stepped across her office with his arm outstretched and hovered over her on the side of her desk.

She jiggled the drawer handle, but it wouldn't open. "I…" Another attempt didn't open it, either. "Laura." She only gave him a brief glance before jerking one more time on the drawer. "I just had this thing open…"

"Can I help?"

"No. No, thank you." She shook her head. "I don't need help from a Kashgar." The fact that she'd said that out loud made her freeze. Her cheeks burned as she stared at the faulty drawer.

"Actually…" Nathan folded his arms. "Part Kashgar. Most of me's human."

Laura forced herself to meet his gaze. He was smirking, which only unsettled her more. A giggle escaped her, and she had no idea why. "Yeah, but the rest of you isn't."

"Hey, look who's talking. You're not even a little human." He unfolded his arms to demonstrate that fact with his thumb and index finger held just centimeters apart, then tucked that hand back into the crook of his opposite elbow again. "Doesn't seem to affect *your* ability to do your job."

"That's…" With a snort, Laura leaned back and pointed at the stuck drawer. *That's irrelevant.* "I just wanna get this drawer open." Her silver ring flashed and the top drawer burst open and flew out of the desk onto the floor. "Woah!"

"No wand?"

She jerked her gaze from the drawer and shot the part-Kashgar a warning glance. "That"—she pointed at him—"is none of your business."

"Hey…" He lifted his hands. "Careful with that thing."

Despite herself, Laura laughed. "I'm not gonna do anything to you."

"Oh, I know." Nathan lifted a finger, and a shimmering silver bubble grew at the end of it. It floated over Laura's desk and down to the floor, where it engulfed the wayward drawer. The bubble lifted the drawer and deposited it back into the empty hole in the desk.

Before the drawer slid shut, Laura shoved her hand through the bubble, popping it, and snatched up the key she'd been after in the first place. She pushed the drawer shut and gazed at him with a raised eyebrow.

"You won't hurt me after I've been so helpful, right?" Nathan pressed his lips together and chuckled through his nose.

"Oh, please. I could've picked up the drawer."

"Yeah, but the point is you didn't *have* to." He spread his arms and grinned.

He is a Mechanic. Or at least part Kashgar. If he's got a grip on magic, maybe he can help with the energy core issue. "Do you know anything about escape pods?"

Nathan laughed. "*What?*"

"I'm talking about on this ship. This whole…big world your people…wait. You *do* know about that, right?"

He snorted. "Of course."

"So…escape pods?"

"There aren't any."

Laura rolled her eyes. "Yeah, but if there *were*, hypothetically, would you know what it looked like? I mean, would you be able to tell which parts have…whatever functions?"

"Hypothetically? Probably."

"Any idea what an energy core would look like?"

He chuckled. "A hypothetical energy core on a hypothetical escape pod? Sure. They're all the same. Hypothetically."

Laura rolled her eyes. "Never mind."

"Okay, hold on. I'm sorry." With a nod, Nathan stepped toward her desk. "I couldn't help it, but I'll be serious."

"Awesome."

"What are you trying to ask me, Laura?"

The sound of her name on his lips almost made her shudder. *What the heck was that?* She swallowed. "I'm trying to find something that *maybe* looks like an energy core. And I have to know what it looks like if I'm going to find it, especially because I'm about ninety-eight-percent sure it's under a building where a lot of innocent people could get hurt if anything goes wrong. And I wanna make sure that when I…take this energy-core-looking thing, I don't end up being the one doing the hurting." She took a deep breath. "So, it's pretty important. Hypothetically." *You're rambling like a witch with underdeveloped social skills, Laura. Hold it together.*

She expected Nathan to laugh, but he didn't; instead, he

set the tips of his fingers on her desk and leaned forward, frowning in thought. "Well, that sounds tricky. But I'll try to say something helpful."

Laura licked her lips and deflated in her chair. "I would really appreciate that."

"First, can I ask what this is actually about?" A gentle smile lifted the corners of his mouth. "Because it's kinda obvious that you're not puttin' *all* the details out there."

"Well, you can ask." *And no matter how incredible that smile is, I still don't trust a Kashgar-human. The less people who know about the Gorafrex, the better.* "But I can't tell you."

Nathan nodded. "Fair enough. Here's my guess. Something that *looks* like an energy core is gonna stand out. Clear of any cables, panels, levers, controls, you name it, just to give it the space to function—the whole *energy* part, right?"

"Right."

"My second guess is you might be worrying too much about whether removing this thing is going to hurt people. I mean, as long as that's not your actual intent..."

"Oh, my god. *No.*" Laura huffed. "It's the opposite."

He grinned and nodded. His brown eyes, tinged with that purple Kashgar aura, sparkled. "See, I *thought* so. Just had to make sure." She snorted. "So, after my supremely educated guesses, I'll tell you what I *do* know."

Here we go. Has he been messing with me this whole time?

Nathan tilted his head and leaned farther toward her. "This ship was designed to maintain balance. Plain and simple. Okay, sure, the system has faults, and now we're all the way out here calling ourselves a planet, but on the structural level, that balance is still the primary function. If that 'energy-core-looking thing' is somewhere with a lot of people, it's probably put there for a reason. I'd wager the ship is gonna do whatever it can to maintain balance, even if what you're trying to do tips the scales *just* a little bit."

A door slammed shut down the hall, causing Laura to realize how intensely he'd held her gaze as he spoke. She blinked, and Nathan straightened.

"How'd I do?" He pounded his fist against his other palm.

"I'm sorry?"

Nathan chuckled. "Was any of that helpful?"

"Uh…yeah, actually." *And completely unexpected.* "That was exactly what I needed to hear."

"Excellent. If you have any more questions I might be able to answer, I'm happy to chat any time."

"Well that's…nice of you." Laura stuck the small key into the lock of the bottom drawer and slid it open just enough to rummage around for a heavy leather-bound book, then she shut the drawer and locked it. "Hopefully, I won't have any more questions."

"Hey, if everything works out, that's a good thing. Maybe just another chat, then. You and me and coffee. Or dinner…"

Is he asking me out? Laura stood and slipped out from behind her desk. "Um…probably not." She skirted past him, slipping the tiny key into her front pocket, and headed for the door. "I'm just *really* busy right now."

Chuckling, Nathan followed her into the hall.

She reached into her office, hit the lights and locked the door.

"Well, if you happen to have some extra free time

floating around, you know where to find me." He looked at her over his shoulder and pointed to his office.

"Yeah, I sure do." Laura nodded, gripping the book tight against her chest. "Thanks for the talk."

"Yep."

She hurried down the hall, feeling like she was back in middle school.

But at least now I have some *idea where to start.*

CHAPTER NINE

Gruene Hall was packed that night. As the country rock band opening for Nickie finished their last song, Emily's phone buzzed in her back pocket. She pulled it out and stared at the text.

'Just pulled up.'

"That's gotta be John," she muttered, stepping away from where she'd watched the opener backstage. She couldn't help but grin when she typed up a reply. "And now I can mess with him."

'Who's this?'

The three little dots in the bottom corner of her screen blinked on, off, and on again, and it took him a really long time to text her one word.

'John...'

Emily laughed.

"Who's that?" Laura asked, peering over her youngest sister's shoulder with wide eyes.

"A friend." Emily butted her out of the way with her shoulder. "Who I invited to come see the show."

"Ooh." Nickie walked past them with her cable bag in one hand, the other clutching her Strat. "What's his name?"

"What? I never said my friend was a *he*."

"Yeah, but you would've already said their name if he was a *she*." Nickie grinned and peeped out onstage where the lead singer of her opener shouted thank you to the crowd.

Chuck walked up, a cable coiled over his shoulder and her guitar stand in the other hand. "Hey, Emily brought a date."

"It's not a date!" She shook her head but smiled. "Oh, crap. I better let him in."

"Yeah, make sure *he* knows that," Nickie shouted.

Emily darted through the other musicians booked to play as Nickie's band, smiling and nodding at them on her way to the back door, then she remembered she hadn't let John know. She stopped and texted *'Come around to the back.'*

She shoved her phone in her pocket and pushed the back door open. Even from here, she heard the excitement rising from the crowd as her sister took the stage. "Never gets old." Grinning, she held the door open and waited.

John walked around the side of the building with his hands shoved into the front pockets of his jeans, looking exactly the way he shouldn't have looked if he didn't want anyone to be suspicious. He kept glancing over his shoulder, then caught sight of Emily waving beside the back door.

"You weren't kidding." He jogged toward her, grinning like a lunatic.

Or a serious fanboy...

"If I was, you would've figure it out pretty quick. Come on."

"Awesome." John hurried inside, and Emily eased the door shut so it only let out a soft click. "So, do you get to, like…sneak right up next to the stage or something? Like special access? They let you right in up the side, or what?"

Emily laughed. "Oh, we get special access."

Nickie's low voice came through the speakers. "Let's get rockin'." The loud first notes of her electric guitar brought a round of cheers and whistling from the crowd.

Emily nodded toward the stage and raised an eyebrow at John. "You're still gonna have to stand, though." He followed her through backstage and behind the curtain with wide eyes and his mouth hanging open.

"You okay with that?" She had to shout over the music now that the band had joined in with her sister.

"Uh…" The fog of disbelief lifted from John's eyes, and he laughed. "I can't even come up with a witty response. This is amazing!"

"I know, right?" She led him farther toward the front of the stage and stopped next to Laura. Her sister glanced at her then at John and smiled. Emily leaned toward him to say, "That's my sister Laura."

"Oh!" He turned to Laura and stuck out his hand. "I'm John."

"Nice to meet you."

"Hey, is this your date?" Chuck nudged Emily's arm and laughed.

Emily shot him a warning glance. "And this is Chuck. He thinks he's funny."

John shook Chuck's hand next. "Yep. I'm her date."

"Hey…" Emily slapped his arm.

"I'm John."

"Glad you made it, John." Chuck pointed at the stage and Nickie stalking all over it, tossing her head as she jammed just like she always did. Perfectly. "Enjoy the show, huh? This is the *best* way to watch it."

"Yeah, I bet."

Chuck nodded, stuck out his tongue at Emily, and headed off to go take care of whatever else he needed to do.

John nudged Emily's arm with his elbow and grinned. "This is so cool. Thank you."

"Totally. Just don't forget how hard I worked to get you in here."

His eyes popped open. "Really?"

"Oh, yeah. I had to go all the way back there and open the door."

John snorted and ran his fingers through his hair. "Good one."

"I know."

Nickie's first song came to an end, and the crowd erupted into cheers. From where they stood, Emily and John could see the packed dance hall, the flashing blue and yellow stage lights, and the exaggerated wink Nickie shot them when she stepped back toward the band to signal for the next song.

"Man, I'm *really* glad you asked me to come."

When Emily looked at him again, laughing, she found him staring at her instead of the stage. *Maybe this is a date…*

. . .

Two and a half hours later—and three beers each, courtesy of Chuck—they were both covered in sweat from dancing, and Emily was riding a pretty excellent buzz. Nickie and the band finished the set with a bang, which was how the final song ended anyway, and the crowd erupted in cheers, screaming, applause, and whistles. Laughing, Emily dropped the pose she'd struck and let a grinning John pull her against him as they shouted along with the crowd from backstage.

Nickie flipped her long, dark hair back as she shot up from crouching over her Strat, sending a fanning spray of sweat arcing behind her. She pumped a fist in the air and yelled back at the crowd.

"How does she *do* that?" John asked, having to shout above the noise.

Emily shrugged, vaguely aware of wrapping her arms around his waist as she watched her sister turn toward the band and pump her fist at the drummer, bassist, keyboardist, and saxophone player. "It's just what she does," she shouted. *Totally Nickie and just a little bit of magic.*

John laughed. "No, I mean how does she play like *that* for an entire show with what she's wearing?"

"Oh!" She barked out a laugh.

"I mean, if I could take off any more clothes right now, I would…"

"Woah…"

He smirked. "Did she think it was gonna be colder in here, or what?"

"Maybe." Emily glanced at her sister's outfit again—a shimmering, gold-copper dress that only came down to the middle of her thighs. But it had a high button-up collar and long, puffy sleeves that clung to her wrists at the end. "She did that on purpose."

"What?"

"It's not that hot out tonight, so she made sure she'd end up sweating like she needs to to slide all over the guitar." Emily wiped her own sweat from her forehead and smoothed away a few strands of wild hair.

"That's insanely awesome," John shouted.

"I know!"

"Thank you so much," Nickie said into the microphone, still panting. She shifted from foot to foot, cradling her guitar, and nodded at the crowd. "You guys are the best. Hey, let's give it up for these legends playing with me tonight, huh? Melvin Rain on the bass." The crowd roared. "Kenneth Johnson on keys. Ronnie Smith blasting into that sax. And Marcus Bryant on drums. Let 'em have it." Whether she was talking to the crowd or the drummer, it didn't matter. The audience exploded, and Marcus rolled out a clashing, five-second drum solo. The band jammed for another few notes, and Nickie joined them before pressing her mouth up to the microphone. "And I'm Nickie Hadstrom. Goodnight!" The short-lived music ended with a bang, and the stage lights flashed before going dark.

The crowd, of course, didn't let up as Nickie and the musicians headed backstage. The house lights went up, and Emily caught a glimpse of her sister's face as Austin's new 'Queen of Blues' stepped off the stage.

Something's wrong.

Nickie's frown looked like she was in a lot of pain, and she clenched her eyes shut. She stumbled toward Ronnie, whose saxophone dropped against his chest and hung by its strap as he steadied Nickie with both hands. "Woah, Nickie. You okay?"

She peered up at him, confused, then smiled weakly and nodded.

Emily and Laura shared a quick glance, and the youngest Hadstrom sister knew they were thinking the same thing.

The drums are back.

"Hey." Chuck rushed toward Nickie and grabbed her shoulders. He nodded at Ronnie, and the man stepped away to join the other musicians farther backstage. "Nickie, you okay?"

She nodded slowly, blinking at him. "Yeah. I'm good. I just...maybe I didn't drink enough water or something."

"Well, that makes sense. Look at you." Chuck smoothed her soaked hair away from her face. "That was incredible."

"Yeah? That felt pretty good."

"It was better than good, babe. You killed it."

Nickie nodded and seemed to pull herself together. She grabbed Chuck's hand, and they headed toward Laura, Emily, and an awestruck John.

"What happened?" Laura asked.

Nickie eyed her with a tired smile. "Just a bad headache."

"Is it one of those...really bad ones?" Laura asked, glancing again at Emily.

Sure looked like it. Emily tried not to appear worried. *And we might be screwed if the Gorafrex goes hunting right now.*

The middle Hadstrom sister shook her head and blinked. "No. For a minute, I thought it was gonna be one of the really bad ones. But it's...going away."

"What you need right now," Chuck said, oblivious that his girlfriend could hear a deadly creature's primal, witch-luring drumbeat inside her head, "is a crapload of water, some food, and to celebrate blowing this place outta the park."

"Yeah." Nickie eyed her sisters and gave them a reassuring nod. She squeezed Chuck's hand. "That sounds awesome."

"All right. Let's get outta here."

"Should we wait for the crew to finish breaking down?"

"Nickie…" Chuck lifted her chin with his fingers. "You look like you're about to pass out, and that ain't happening."

She laughed and turned toward John, wiggling her eyebrows. "My manager's a real hard-ass."

John chuckled, but his mouth hung open like *he* was about to pass out. "Great show…"

"Thanks, man." Nickie let Chuck lead her toward the back door, and she called over her shoulder, "Hey, it's up to Emily, but you should come with us."

Emily rolled her eyes at her sister, who laughed and turned around in private conversation with Chuck. *Oh, good. Like I can say no after she just invited him.*

"Wait…" John blinked, then looked at Emily with wide eyes. "Did I just get an invite from Nickie Hadstrom to an afterparty?"

Emily smirked. "You wanna come, or what?"

"I think this is the best night of my life."

"I wouldn't call it that. Not yet…" Laura said, pausing beside them on her way to the back door. "The night's not over." She shot a warning glance at Emily, then headed after Nickie and Chuck to the rear lot.

That was unnecessary. Emily shrugged and shook her head, trying to explain away her sister's mood. "That's Laura..."

"Yeah, you weren't kidding when you called her serious."

"She's just got a lot on her mind. A few drinks'll loosen her up." *I hope.* She cocked her head and grinned. "You're still totally invited, by the way."

"Cool." John laughed. "I'm still totally down."

CHAPTER TEN

They stayed out at Inferno's through last call, and Nickie thought it was exactly what they all needed. Chuck had ordered her a massive burger, and she'd had her water refilled twice before she felt right enough to order a beer. Laura's two and a half margaritas put a real smile on her face, and while it was weird to see Emily out with another guy less than two weeks after breaking up with Jeremy, her sister looked exceptionally happy. Or maybe it was the beer.

When the bar closed and everyone got kicked out, the Hadstrom sisters, Chuck, and John headed to the parking lot. "All right," Chuck said, turning to walk backward toward his car. "Who here can't drive home? Besides Laura."

Laura snorted and pointed at him, but failed to come up with a retort.

Emily laughed. "Definitely me."

"Well, good. We got you covered. John, what about you?"

"I'm good, man. Only had one drink after the show."

"You sure? We can cram five people in my car…"

Nickie drew in a loud breath. "Didn't we fit six one time?"

"Yeah!" Emily pointed at Laura. "When your friend… what was her name?"

"Daisy?" Nickie offered.

"Yeah, *Daisy*. That woman was nuts."

"Woah, woah. Okay." Laura raised her hands, laughing. "First of all, Daisy is *not* my friend. She's a junior instructor, and Chuck offered to give her a ride."

Emily laughed. "She was still crazy."

"I know."

"So anyway!" Chuck clapped his hands, and the sisters burst out laughing. "John, you sure you're good? Austin's not exactly around the corner."

"It's only an hour." John pulled his keys out of his back pocket. "I had to drive to Lubbock a few months ago after closing the last restaurant I worked at. Made that just fine."

"That sounds like the worst drive ever," Nickie said, stepping up to the passenger-side door of Chuck's car.

"It was great, actually. Nobody on the road. And I *almost* got to see the sunrise, so…" He shrugged and jerked his thumb back toward his silver Toyota.

"All right. Well, thanks for comin' out, man." Chuck shook John's hand. "Great to meet you."

"Yeah, you too. Nickie, great show. Really. It was awesome."

Nickie grinned. *Jeremy never came to my shows. So there's a point for the new guy.* "Thank you," she said with a wave.

"You should come to the next one. On…" She glanced at Chuck.

"I dunno. Thursday, I think? I'll hafta check."

"Yeah, whenever it is, I'll ask Emily to sneak me in again. Good to meet you, too, Laura."

Laura had already opened the backseat of Chuck's car and climbed halfway through it. "Later, gator!" She stuck a hand behind her and waved.

Nickie leaned against the passenger-side door and watched her rarely drunk older sister fumble with the wrong seatbelt. *At least she's not seriously uptight anymore…*

"Hey, guys," Emily said, drifting slowly with John toward his truck. "Just a few minutes. I'll be right there."

"Yeah, yeah." Chuck waved a dismissive hand and opened the driver-side door. "You have two minutes."

Nickie rolled her eyes and whispered at him over the top of the car. "Five minutes."

"*Five* minutes!" He grinned, then jerked open the door and slid behind the wheel.

Opening her own door, Nickie watched Emily and John walk toward his truck with very little space between them. *Not yet, anyway.*

"Hey." Chuck ducked his head to meet her gaze through the open door. "Did you say five minutes just so you could spy on them?"

She laughed and got into the passenger seat. "Absolutely not. That's something our mom would do."

"That's something she *did* do," Laura said from the backseat.

"Wait, *what*?"

"Oh, yeah. With Emily and Jeremy, and with you…

guys…" The oldest Hadstrom sister still hadn't figured out her seatbelt predicament, jamming the clip over and over into the wrong buckle.

"Laura. You got the wrong. Oh, jeeze." Nickie crawled over the center console to help Laura find the right buckle.

"Your mom used to spy on us?" Chuck asked, squinting into the rearview mirror.

"When you first started dating, yeah." Laura nodded, closed her eyes, and dropped her head against the seat. "She thought it was funny."

"*What?*" Nickie glanced at Chuck, and they cracked up.

"Glad we're so amusing. I mean, this *is* the entertainment industry, right?"

Nickie snorted and glanced back at her sister. Laura's mouth had popped open, and a little snore escaped her. "Jeeze, not even three drinks. She probably just made all that up."

"I dunno, babe. She's never really been a good liar, has she?"

"I mean, except for when she's drunk…"

The door behind Chuck clicked open, and Emily jumped in beside her sister. "Okay, let's go—woah." She laughed at the sight of Laura passed out. "That was fast."

"She doesn't get out much, does she?" Chuck started the engine.

"Not like this…" Nickie strapped her seatbelt on and glanced at Emily. "John's pretty cool."

"Yep." Emily smiled out the window as they left the bar parking lot and headed for I-35 back to Austin.

"That's it?" Chuck laughed and looked up at the rearview mirror. "Just yep?"

"I agree?" Emily spread her arms. "There wasn't a question."

Chuck glanced at Nickie and stuck his thumb over his shoulder. "Master of evasion back there."

Nickie smirked and shook her head. "Where'd you meet him?"

"Meadowlark."

"You work together, huh?" Chuck tilted his head. "Doesn't that make things kinda...sticky?"

"*Sticky?*" Nickie shot him in incredulous glance.

"You know, if things don't work out."

"There's not even anything to work out, Chuck." Emily dropped her head against the seat.

"Definitely looked like something..."

"Okay, remind me which one came first, man. You dating Nickie or you becoming her manager?"

Nickie laughed. "You guys are ridiculous."

"Just friendly banter, babe." Chuck made a face at Emily through the rearview mirror, and she shot one back. "And Emily gets a point for that one."

Nickie turned around to wink at her younger sister, and Emily shot her a sarcastic thumbs up before turning to stare out the window. *Yeah, there's something there. Or she'd be talking a lot more than this.*

Chuck pulled up in front of their giant, Victorian-style house on Pressler Street a little after 2:00 a.m. He shifted into park, sighed, and turned around to look at Nickie's sisters in the back seat. "Is this what having kids is gonna look like?"

Nickie laughed. "I didn't know we were having kids, Chuck."

His head whipped toward her, and he blinked. "That's not what I…I'm not…"

"Oh, my god. Relax." Grinning, she looked at Emily and Laura passed out in the backseat, leaning against their prospective doors. "This is what having two passed-out sisters looks like."

"You want any help?"

"Nope. Emily can pull it together."

"Okay…" He popped the trunk, then leaned toward her over the center console. "Come here."

Nickie grabbed his face and kissed him, which made her wish she could end the night like this instead of helping at least one drunk sister up two different flights of stairs.

"Great show tonight," he whispered. "You're always amazing. Tonight was even better."

"Thank you." She bit her lip, smiled, and opened the passenger-side door. "Drive safe, okay?"

"I always do."

After she'd shut the door, Nickie stepped around the car to get to the backseat. Emily woke up the minute she lost her makeshift headrest. She grunted, jerking straight up and blinking wide eyes. "Already?"

"Yep. I need your help with our rational, responsible, always level-headed sister." Nickie nodded toward Laura.

"Yeesh." Emily groaned and slapped the back of the driver's seat. "Thanks for the ride, Chuck."

"Thanks for not pukin' in my car, Em."

"I didn't drink *that* much." She rolled her eyes and

leaned over to unbuckle Laura's seatbelt, then she pulled herself out of the car as Nickie dropped her Strat's guitar strap over her head. The trunk closed with a *thunk*, and together they worked to wake Laura up enough to put most of her weight on her own feet.

"'Night, babe." Nickie blew Chuck a kiss through the window.

"'Night." His taillights had almost disappeared by the time they got Laura up the first set up cement steps up the hill toward the house.

"I'm *fine*," Laura muttered, unprompted.

"Yeah, we know." Emily grunted. "Could you maybe not pull my hair, though?"

They got through the front door and paused at the huge staircase at the end of the foyer. "I don't know if we can make it up there," Nickie said.

"Oh...and she's got those stupid wards around her room." Emily rolled her eyes. "I'm not even gonna try to mess with those."

Laura lurched forward out of their grasp, bumping against Nickie's guitar over her shoulder and almost whacking her in the face with its neck. "Hey, *careful...*"

"You know what's stupid?" Their older sister whipped a finger at the floor. "Those stairs. I hate them." Spinning on the toes of her hiking boots, she wobbled toward the living room and plummeted face-first onto the couch.

The dog door off the mudroom in the back opened and closed with a click. Speed trotted into the living room, his tongue drooping out of his mouth. "Hey, buddy." Emily crouched to greet him. The chubby bulldog ignored her and leapt up onto the couch to curl between

Laura's legs and the back cushion. "He doesn't sleep with *her.*"

"Guess they're both walkin' on the wild side tonight," Nickie said.

"Not sure I'm into that kinda betrayal." Emily folded her arms. "That dog's been…"

Nickie knew her sister was still talking, but all the words blended into one low drone. She blinked, trying to push through the intense pressure building in her temple. *Please not again. Not now.* A rushing filled her ears, and the increasing thump of her own heartbeat morphed into the loud, fast pounding of the Gorafrex's ancient drumming. A bright, flashing pain flared behind her eyes, and she hardly felt the cold wood of the staircase banister beneath her fingers. Then, just like that, the drumming stopped and the pain receded. Nickie realized she'd been holding her breath.

"*Hey.*" Emily grabbed her shoulder. "Why won't you answer me?"

"What?"

"You just went totally white. I thought you were gonna fall over." Frowning, Emily leaned forward to meet her sister's gaze. "Headache again?"

"Yeah."

"Is it the drums?"

Until I start hearing them and they don't *stop, I don't need to worry her or Laura for no reason.* "No. No drums. I dunno. Maybe the show took more outta me than I thought."

"Yeah, maybe. You should take something."

"I have aspirin in my room. I'm just gonna go to bed, okay?" Nickie gave her sister a tired smile and lifted her guitar strap over her head before handing over the Strat. "Can you set this on the chair or something?"

"Yeah." Emily took the guitar into the living room and hurried back. "Can I do anything to help?"

"No. I'll feel better in the morning."

"You sure you're okay?"

"Yep." Nickie started up the stairs, keeping her hand on the banister. "'Night, Em."

Emily followed behind her. "Don't make it weird. I'm comin' up too."

Once she'd closed her bedroom door, Nickie pulled her keys out of her back pocket and fingered the coin-sized keyring. Her sisters had the exact same thing on their keys; the only difference was the magically engraved thumbprint in the center of each coin, specific to each one of them.

She slipped her boots off and didn't bother with her short, long-sleeved dress. She rolled onto her bed and closed her eyes. "Just in case," she whispered, closing her fingers over the thumbprint coin, knowing it allowed her access to the one place she knew was safe. "If the drums come back, I'll just go sleep in the Clubhouse."

CHAPTER ELEVEN

Nickie and Emily sat at the kitchen table, both on their second cups of coffee, when Laura tromped through the mudroom at the back of the house and into the kitchen. "What time is it?"

"Hey. Good morning." Nickie raised her mug with a tired smirk. "How's your head?"

"I asked what time—"

Emily turned to glance at the clock over the stove. "Almost nine-thirty."

Laura blinked. "And neither one of you thought it was a good idea to wake me up at a reasonable hour?"

"Laura, you passed out on the couch at two o'clock this morning," Nickie said, putting her cup down. "This *is* a reasonable hour."

"I haven't gotten anything ready, and I haven't told you guys the plan, and we're supposed to be going to the Thinkery today to grab that stupid—" With a grunt of frustration, Laura whirled from the kitchen and rushed into the dining room, her footsteps thundering above her sisters' heads as she stormed upstairs.

Emily snorted. "She's already made a plan."

"Of course she has. She texted you about the Thinkery, right?"

"And told me one of those energy cores is under the children's museum? Oh, yeah. Definitely got that text."

A door slammed, and Laura's footsteps stomped back down. She took more time returning to the kitchen, then she entered and stopped in front of them. "Sorry."

"Totally cool," Nickie said.

"Happens to the best of us." Emily nodded and sipped at her coffee. "Whatcha got there?"

Laura glanced down at her arms. "It's a book."

"No…"

Nickie shot her younger sister a glance. "How 'bout you put the book down, grab some coffee, and explain this plan of yours."

"It's not *my* plan." Laura hesitantly set the book on the table, keeping her hand atop it, and glanced at them. "I mean, yes, I came up with it. With a little bit of help. But we're *all* going together, so that makes it *our* plan. Got it?"

"Okay, sure." Nickie shrugged.

"Maybe get that coffee, huh?"

"Yeah." Laura peered at the huge book, slowly withdrew her fingers, and nodded. "Yeah, coffee." She took off across the kitchen toward the coffeepot.

Emily leaned over the table and tried to read the title on the front of the leather-bound book upside down, but the words were too faded. *Where did* this *thing come from?*

Nickie bumped her foot against Emily's under the table. "You wanna get yelled at again for stealing her thunder?"

"What?"

"She *has a plan*, Em. Just let her do her thing."

"Have you seen this before?"

"That book," Laura called from the other side of the kitchen, stirring sugar and cream into her coffee, "came from a Swedish historian in the eighteenth century."

"Okay. But you didn't get it in Sweden." Emily glanced over her shoulder and raised an eyebrow.

Laura took her first sip and let out a grateful sigh. "No. I didn't get it from Sweden. I got it from—"

"Carl Hopkins," Emily and Nickie said at the same time.

"Yeah, yeah." The youngest Hadstrom witch turned back around in her chair. "You get *everything* from Carl."

"You guys just know everything, don't you?"

Emily stared at her coffee. *She doesn't say that unless she's about to prove that we don't...*

Laura sat at the table and took another sip. "Actually, this was a present."

"A present?" Nickie frowned at the book.

"Roger gave it to me."

Laura's sisters shared a groan. "That guy would've ripped out his heart and given it to you," Emily said.

Nickie snorted. "I wouldn't be surprised if he'd already tried it. More than once."

"That's ridiculous." Laura put her coffee aside and pulled the huge book toward her. "Roger's an archaeologist and a colleague."

Emily pursed her lips. "So, he just said, 'Here, Laura. I

was about to toss this piece-of-junk book I don't need anymore, but you can have it if you want'?"

"That's not how most people give gifts, Em."

"Didn't he take a university job somewhere else?" Nickie frowned at the book.

Emily leaned over the table. "Because *you* kept rejecting him?"

"Okay, fine." Laura blinked. A blush rose in her cheeks. "He was in love with me, and this book was one of his most valuable finds of Peabrain magic in Europe and, yes, he took another job because I didn't want to go out with him. Ever. He was really…short."

Emily barked out a laugh. "You shortist! *That's* why you wouldn't give the guy one date?"

"No, that's *not* why. There were other reasons…"

"But you kept the book." Nickie held her older sister's gaze, her lips pressed tightly together in confusion. She folded her arms in mock judgement.

"Of course I kept it. Do you know how rare it is to find anything like this strictly devoted to Peabrain magic? I mean, even beyond the fact that since before the Middle Ages, they've forgotten who they are and what they can do."

"Yeah, they're probably the reason *for* the Middle Ages —wait." Emily squinted at the book beneath her sister's hand and pointed at it. "That's a Peabrain spellbook?"

Laura shrugged. "More or less."

"And now you're gonna tell us we have to use it to get into the museum's basement, or wherever that energy core is. Right?"

"Yes, Em. That's exactly what I was about to do."

Shaking her head, Laura opened the hardbound cover of the four-hundred-year-old spellbook, which creaked at the movement. "I hope it's as satisfying for you to guess everything as it would've been for me to tell you about it."

"Sorry to burst your bubble." Emily snorted. "Get it? Bubble. 'Cause that's a book of…" When she looked up at Nickie to share the joke with the one sister who actually appreciated her sense of humor more often than not, Nickie just eyed her sideways and shook her head. Then she closed her eyes, and a tiny smile twitched at the corner of her mouth. *She thinks it's funny. Guess my timing's just off.* Emily cleared her throat and looked at Laura. "Sorry. For real. I won't keep trying to guess." *Not out loud.*

Laura's gaze flicked toward her youngest sister, then down to the spellbook's brittle, yellowing pages. "Thank you." She sifted through it, then tilted her head and took a deep breath. "I've only looked through this thing a few times. Never really had the opportunity to really study it. Or the need to, actually."

Again, Emily tried to read the words on the page upside down, but the handwriting scrawled in large, flowery loops, just made her dizzy. *I bet this is how she talks to her students, too.*

"I stopped by the university yesterday to grab this, and to see if anyone there had an idea for how to get into the Thinkery without being seen; plus, hopefully figure out the best way to dismantle that core without damaging the building or anyone in it." Laura's frown darkened as she skimmed the pages.

"Why would it damage the building?" Emily asked.

"Well…" Laura frowned, nodding at herself or the book

or both. "The escape pod around that prison is pretty much supporting the infrastructure of Austin at this point. Maybe more."

"Yeah. *Underground.*"

"Where do you think earthquakes happen, Em? Or volcanoes. Tsunamis. Sinkholes are a thing too."

Emily shrugged. "Is it really *that* much of a supporting structure?"

"I don't know. I'm trying to avoid us having to find out."

Nickie and Emily exchanged glances, and Nickie shrugged.

"I also think it's best to use as little of our magic as we can," Laura added. "You know, so the Gorafrex doesn't, I don't know, smell what we're up to or something."

Nickie snorted. "So Peabrain magic is the best way to go?"

"Maybe. If we have to. Winston's idea seemed pretty sound."

Nickie turned her head to the side and rubbed at the back of her neck. "You didn't tell him what's going on, did you?"

"Come on, Nickie. I know how to be careful. I only gave him a vague summary."

Emily raised her hand. "Who's Winston?" *I'm the last one to know everything.*

Nickie glanced at her. "An elf."

"Who happens to be an archaeology professor," Laura added.

"Oh, the elf who was *your* professor before you started working there, right?"

"Yeah, Em. Most of them were my professors before I

started working there." Laura swallowed, took another sip of coffee, and finally found what she was looking for. "Okay, here it is. We're gonna use a transport bubble to get…under the children's museum."

"No way." Emily grinned. "That's one of the coolest things they can do."

"It's not just Peabrains. Witches can handle a transport bubble too." Laura's lips turned up in a small, satisfied smile. "I just haven't ever really tried to do this before, so we need a little bit of practice first."

"For real? We're gonna do this right now?"

"Yep." Laura smoothed down the pages of the book and stood. "As soon as we get it perfect, we're gonna go give that energy core a good smashing." Nickie and Emily burst into laughter. "What's so funny?"

"*A good smashing?*" Nickie grinned. "When did you start talking like that?"

Laura rolled her eyes. "That's what Rutilda kept saying."

"Yeah, I think I woulda liked her." Emily stood, and Nickie followed. "So how do we do this?"

"Okay. There's the spell word to summon the bubble. Then we all step inside it and think about the exact place we wanna go."

"Sounds easy enough." Nickie nodded.

"Well, just to be on the safe side, we should practice."

"Of course." Emily nodded. "Scientific process and all that."

Laura shot her a perturbed glance, then walked around the table to join them. "Let's start with something simple. Like the back yard."

Emily gestured toward the mudroom. "But we could just walk right out the door—"

Nickie jabbed her little sister in the ribs.

Emily chuckled. "Okay, sorry. I'm done. Are we talking about the middle of the back yard or, like, right outside the door?"

Closing her eyes, Laura sighed. "Let's just say outside the door. Ready?" Her sisters nodded. "Okay. *Conmeatus.*" She lifted her hand away from her thigh, and the silver ring on her thumb flashed.

A pearly, opalescent bubble formed, growing larger and larger on her ring until it disconnected and kept growing. Laura stepped inside, then beckoned her sisters to follow. Nickie stepped through the shimmering wall, then Emily, and right before her second foot left the kitchen floor to enter the bubble, Speed zipped around the corner, leapt into the shimmering sphere with them, and then they all disappeared.

CHAPTER TWELVE

The opalescent bubble burst around them, and they most definitely weren't in the back yard. With a snort, Speed jumped up onto the bed beside the wall. Laura folded her arms. "So, I *would* ask who wasn't thinking about going into the back yard, but seeing as we're in your *room*, Em…"

Emily shrugged, grinning. "Sorry."

"Why were thinking about your room?" Nickie asked.

The youngest Hadstrom sister took two huge steps toward the bedside table, stretched forward to snatch her phone, and returned. "I didn't even mean to, guys. Just hopin' I didn't miss a text or anything."

Laura scoffed. "Did you?"

"What? Oh, no. I didn't."

With a soft chuckle, Nickie shook her head.

"Wow." Laura sighed. "Okay, Em. Your turn."

"Huh?"

"Cast the spell. Make us a transport bubble, and this time, we're *going* into the back yard."

"Okay, okay." Emily stretched out her hand and stared at the copper ring on her thumb. "What's the spell again?"

"Seriously?"

"*Conmeatus*," Nickie whispered.

"*Conmeatus*." Emily grinned when another pearly bubble grew from the top of her ring and disconnected. "I *really* like not having to take out a wand every time I wanna do something."

"Emily, focus," Laura muttered.

"Right." When the bubble was large enough, the Hadstrom sisters stepped inside. Emily turned to look at Speed, who'd curled up on her bed and looked very much asleep. "Speed? Come on, buddy. You wanna go outside?" The immortal bulldog didn't even twitch. "Oh, I get it." Emily smirked. "Freeloader." The bubble disappeared.

When it burst again, they were standing outside their back door off the mudroom. The sun beat down on them hot and bright, the humidity already overwhelming, and they blinked at their open lawn at the top of the hill, surrounded by the black iron fence they'd torn apart a week ago to forge their iron, Gorafrex-vanquishing weapons.

"We *have* to fix that fence." Laura nodded at the gaping hole in the elaborate wrought iron that had come with the house when they bought it.

"Probably not that high on the priority list, though, right?" Nickie chuckled.

"No. Not right now." For the first time that morning, Laura smiled. "That was really good, you guys. I won't say we mastered a Peabrain spell, but almost."

"I mean, it *is* really easy." Emily shrugged.

"Yeah, as long as you don't start daydreaming about John again and take us somewhere else." Nickie folded her arms and raised an eyebrow.

Emily puffed out a breath. "I wasn't thinking about John…"

"Hmm. Then whose texts were you trying not to miss?"

"I…just any text."

"Yeah, okay."

"Hey, we're on a time crunch, remember?" Laura spread her arms. "Yeah, this is a learning process while we figure out how to do this right, but we have to do it right. And then we *really* have to be quick about destroying those energy cores before the Gorafrex gets to them. So, let's focus. Please." Laura's urgent tone left her sisters speechless for a moment, then they nodded.

"Yeah, okay."

"You're right, Laura. Let's do this. What's next?"

Laura nodded. "Anybody have any ship-destroying tools tucked away somewhere?"

"Oh." Emily grinned. "Does this mean I get to use that *Excsindo* spell again?"

"*Woah…*" Nickie tossed up her hands.

"Emily," Laura spat in a harsh whisper, then glanced at the neighboring houses. Her gaze lingered a little longer on the back porch of the house behind them, whose owner had almost caught them in the act of casting that same spell the day they made their iron weapons. "You can't just go shouting spells for the fun of it. Not with these rings. A wand takes a lot more intention to cast any kind of magic, but these are…"

"They're trigger-happy, Em." Nickie nodded at her. "I'm

pretty sure you've already figured out we have to focus a lot more on *not* using the rings than using them."

"Jeeze. I'm sorry." Emily tried to look apologetic, but she couldn't help a tiny smile of excitement. "I'm not gonna cast that spell *now*. Come on." She folded her arms. "It's not like I'm twelve and just got my wand. I have a whole decade of practice under my belt."

"Not with your ring, you don't." Laura frowned and glanced at the copper ring on her sister's thumb.

"So? Can I use that spell or not?"

The two older ones stared at their reckless sister.

"Probably not, Em," Nickie muttered.

"We don't know how much stronger it'd be with your ring instead of your wand," Laura said. "And Rutilda said a combination of magic and physical…"

Emily cocked her head. "Don't say smashing."

"Destruction, okay? The Engineer said both of those together give us the best chance of destroying the energy cores, so we just need some really effective tools for breaking things."

"Let's check the basement," Nickie offered. Emily nodded.

"Okay. Good opportunity to practice again. You take this one, Nick."

"Me?"

Emily smirked at her sister. "Hey, we started with the back yard. Yours is a step up."

Nickie chuckled. "Fine." She flicked her hand out and muttered, "*Conmeatus*." The black legacy ring on her thumb flashed with a dark light, and another shimmering transport bubble bloomed on the band. It floated amidst them and grew. The sisters stepped into it, each thinking specifically about the basement.

When the bubble popped, they'd made it. "Woah!" Emily's arms flailed as her feet slipped over the scattered fishing poles lying where she'd landed. She staggered forward, almost fell, and crouched to catch herself with her hands. She hopped up and spun around, walking backward. "Who the heck left fishing poles in the middle of the basement? Since when do we even *have* fishing poles?"

Nickie bent to pick them up—three shorter-than-average poles with the bobs tied to the line, dangling against each other. "I think these are the ones Dad gave us."

"My freshman year of high school?" Laura asked. "I definitely didn't take mine with me when I moved out."

"Yeah, I *know* I left mine." Emily scowled at the poles in her sister's hands and shook her head.

"Mom and Dad *did* help us move in, though." Nickie headed toward the side wall lined with metal shelves. She couldn't find a space big enough for the poles in all the haphazardly piled tools, papers, boxes, and knickknacks, so she set them upright between two of the metal shelving units and called it good. "How much you wanna bet Dad brought these and snuck them in?"

Emily snickered. "That's something Dad would do. Probably forgot all about it, too."

"I mean, they *did* split up right after we bought this place." Nickie wrinkled her nose. "He probably forgot about a lot of stuff."

"This place is a mess." Laura stepped over the scattered, half-opened boxes of extra bedding they'd never use. A bicycle lay on its side in front of her. She discerned its back wheel and narrowed her eyes. The wheel was spinning. "Guys, I think someone's in here," she said low.

"What?" Nickie whirled.

Laura pointed at the bike.

Emily froze. "Oh, no."

"Oh, no *what*, Em?"

The youngest Hadstrom sister shot the others a grimace, then headed toward the gray plastic tote against the wall. At the very bottom of the storage bin, a tiny door about six inches tall was open and spilling a bright golden glow onto the basement floor. "I could've sworn I shut this last time."

"Oh, great." Laura tossed her hands up, then dropped them against her thighs. "We're about to go break an energy core to stop the Gorafrex from destroying the *entire* ship, or at least Austin, and now we have a frigging *teezler* problem, too?"

"I think you're blowing this outta proportion." Nickie scanned the shelving units, looking for anything that might bash loose an energy core. *Or at least bash it in...* "They're honestly pretty harmless."

"Only if you don't actually care about any of your stuff." Laura squinted at the basement ceiling, which was so far above them that she could hardly see it.

Emily dropped down on all fours in front of the gray tote and peered through the doorway. "I don't think there's a problem. After they weaseled their way out of their pen, I'm pretty sure they got it out of their system. Didn't you, you crazy little spazzballs?" Through the doorway, a number of tiny, puffy round creatures with shocks of white fur jumped and pranced around in the miniature, magical version of a bright-green, sprawling meadow. They squeaked at each other, rolling and bouncing. Emily lifted a hand to wiggle her fingers at them in a wave.

From the ceiling, a teezler scurried down an electricity cable, hopped down a shelving unit, and rolled in a zig-zag toward Emily. It stopped just behind the unsuspecting witch and pulled a mocking face at its fellows inside the tote.

"Did you guys figure out how to escape all on your own?" Emily asked in a cooing voice.

The teezlers jumped and squeaked, keeping the witch's attention as their rogue comrade scurried up her shoe, the back of her thigh, and over the waistline of her jeans. Two of the teezlers inside the pen started wrestling.

"And you all decided to come right back home after you had your fun?" Emily squinted at them, but she couldn't help smiling when the furry troublemakers all nodded and blinked wide, falsely innocent eyes. "That was incredibly mature of you." She reached up to scratch an itch on her back, almost swiping the escaped teezler without knowing it. The little creature leapt aside and clung to the back of her shirt. "Okay, you guys. I'm shutting the door, and I'm gonna block you in. No more escaping."

The tiny creatures squeaked and chattered at her, nodding and hugging each other. One of them let out a huge yawn and shivered, bristling its fur as it nestled down in front of the door for a much-needed nap. Emily stood, chuckling, and the teezler clinging to her shirt managed a vigorous wave at the others before the witch closed the door with the toe of her shoe. The golden light winked out, and the door almost disappeared into the plastic siding of the tote.

"You know, until we had to start taking care of teezlers, I really didn't understand how anyone could get away with whatever they wanted just by being cute." Emily tugged a crate of netting toward the gray tote and nestled it right up against the door. "You guys have any idea what all these nets are for?"

Nickie shrugged.

"I'm pretty sure that was the point Nanna was making when she gave them to us," Laura said.

"The nets?"

"The teezlers, Em."

"Oh. Yeah, probably." Emily stood and clapped the dust off her hands.

"Hey, did you guys even know we had this?" With both hands, Nickie tugged on the hilt of a sword wedged into a huge pile of old shoes on one of the shelves. It came free with a loud, metallic ring, and she pointed the broadsword at the ceiling. The weight of it caught her off guard, though, and the point clanged down on the cement floor.

"Nickie!" Laura hurried toward her with wide eyes. "What are you doing?"

"I mean, it's not quite *Sword in the Stone* or anything, but that was really hard to get out of there."

Emily barked out a laugh.

"You think this would work for bashing up some energy cores?" Nickie lifted the sword again, but she could only get it up to a ninety-degree angle before it clanged to the floor.

"That's not funny. I'm pretty sure it's one of our family heirlooms."

"Witches used swords?" Emily asked, joining them.

"And wizards, yeah." Laura glanced at Nickie trying to lift the sword yet again. "Just because we have magic doesn't mean we don't use what everybody else uses. I mean, we have cell phones. And a microwave."

Emily wrinkled her nose. "Which we shouldn't even have. Do you know how much those things *ruin* your food?"

"Okay, this is ridiculous. *Recursus*." Laura pointed at the sword, and the minute her silver ring flashed, the weapon jerked out of Nickie's hands and sailed across the basement to settle upright against the wall beside the fishing rods.

"Not cool." Nickie frowned.

"Well, we've got some heavy destruction tools to find, and you're over here playing King Arthur."

Nickie and Emily sniggered, then Emily's eyes widened, and she pointed at a shelf on the other side of the basement. "What about *that*?"

Her sisters turned to see the bowling bag on the second-to-top shelf. The letters printed on the side had faded over the years, but they were still clear from where the witches stood—*Magic 14.*

"Oh, my god." Laura's hands went to her face as she stared at the bag.

Nickie cracked up laughing.

"Dad's sense of humor was *epic* when we were kids," Emily said, grinning. "And we had no *idea*."

"Honestly, Em, that might be a really good choice."

"I can use it?" Emily shot her oldest sister a wide-eyed, hopeful glance. "For real?"

Laura shrugged. "Uh…go for it." She chuckled. "You look like you're about to run away screaming."

"Yeah, for your bowling ball. To use as a *wrecking* ball." Emily darted toward the shelf. She couldn't quite reach the handle of the bag, so she pointed at it. "*Venio.*"

The bag jerked off the shelf and dropped to the ground with a *thump*, followed by a few loose screws and a box of nickel Jacks, the silver game pieces scattering across the floor. "Woah." Emily pressed against the edge of the metal shelving unit as it wobbled, threatening to fall over on her. It finally settled.

Laura shook her head. "You're almost as bad as the teezlers."

Emily picked up the bowling bag. "Yeah, but I don't do it on purpose." Grinning, she lugged the bag toward Laura. "Seriously, I'm just surprised you're letting me touch this thing. It was, like, your prized possession when we were kids."

Laura smirked. "Just one. And that's because you and Nickie *hated* bowling. Whenever we went, it was just him and me."

"You should start going again. Maybe join a league or something, right?"

"Absolutely not."

"It's good to have hobbies that aren't related to work, Laura." Nickie crossed the basement from the other side, the long handle of a sledgehammer clenched in her hands.

"It's true." Emily grunted and slung the bowling bag's straps over her shoulder.

"Oh, come on." Laura folded her arms and glanced between them. "Both of you *work* with your boyfriends."

"John is *not* my boyfriend." Emily wrinkled her nose. "I just met him."

Nickie stepped behind the sledgehammer head resting on the ground and paused, her mouth open. "Yeah, I got nothing." She swung the hammer up and settled the handle over her shoulder. "But at least I read for fun. And none of those books have anything to do with music. Or Chuck."

"Okay, let's drop talking about my hobbies, huh?" Laura glanced at the pseudo-tools her sisters carried and cocked her head. "Maybe you guys should put those somewhere safe until we *find* the energy core. 'Cause Em, honestly, I have an image of you dropping that thing in the worst place possible and really getting us into trouble."

"Hey, I would *not*. What about Nickie?"

"Nickie isn't nearly as excited about destroying an ancient piece of machinery."

Nickie sighed. "This thing is really heavy." She dropped the sledgehammer from her shoulder with a dull *thud*. "What're you gonna use?"

Laura grinned. "Mine's in the Clubhouse. There is no *way* I could carry it *and* climb out of that manhole to the Engineer's cavern."

"Hey, that's a great idea." Emily blinked. "My keys are in my room."

"Yeah, mine too." Nickie shared a sly glance with her sister before they both muttered, "*Claves*." Their rings flashed, and Emily laughed.

"Seriously?" Laura pursed her lips.

Her sisters shrugged at the same time. A short, muffled

banging came up upstairs, following by a few more dull *thumps* and the jingling of keys. Both sisters glanced up at the high basement ceiling above

Laura rolled her eyes. "Oh, fine. *Claves.*" Then her ring flashed, too, and the jingling of keys grew louder. Something thumped on the floor above them, and they heard Speed let out a few sharp yips.

Emily smirked. "You think he likes that?"

"I think he's pissed a bunch of flying keys woke him up." Laura folded her arms, but she smiled. A series of thuds came from the basement door, and Laura muttered, "*Patentibus.*" The door flew open with a *bang*, and three jingling silver streaks shot across the room toward them.

Each witch raised her hand to catch her own set of keys. Nickie set her thumb onto the thumbprint in the coin and disappeared. Grinning, Emily pressed the silver coin on her keyring and vanished too. Laura grumbled and fiddled with her keys. "Jeeze, why do I have so *many?*" Then she pressed her thumb into the perfect indentation of her print on the coin and vanished after her sisters.

CHAPTER THIRTEEN

Laura appeared in the center of the one-room Clubhouse just as Emily tossed the bowling bag into the ratty, frayed armchair across from the cherry-red futon. "You know, now that I think about it, this place is like one giant purse."

"*Please* don't say that, Em." Laura turned and walked around the futon to the coffee table set against the wall beside the bookshelf. "Because then you're gonna try to use it like a purse, and I don't wanna have to go through your mess every time we come here." An origami dragon leapt from the bookshelf and soared toward her, paper claws reaching for her hair. She ducked the playful attack and grabbed the massive, incredibly heavy socket wrench Rutilda the Engineer gave her two nights ago. With a grunt, she hefted it over her shoulder and returned to her sisters. "Which seems to be a lot more, lately."

"Don't say it like it's such a bad thing." Nickie dropped onto the futon and propped the sledgehammer against the armrest. "This *is* the only place we know that stops the drums in my head. Probably stops the Gorafrex, too."

"It'd be really great if we don't ever get a chance to test that theory," Emily pointed out as she sat on the arm of the old chair with the bowling bag.

"Okay, don't get too comfortable." Laura sat in the other armchair—upholstered in the ugliest combination of bright-red, lemon-yellow, and faded mint-green plaid. "We're dropping these things off, then getting right back to it. Yeah?"

"Yeah, okay."

Nickie crossed her legs, a foot dangling in the air over the other. "So that's really it? We go in with a transport bubble, pop back into the Clubhouse to grab our weapons of destruction, go back, break the thing or disconnect it or whatever, and that's it?"

"Pretty much." Laura cocked her head. "I worry, though, how breaking the core might affect the museum…and all the…" She frowned.

"All the kids?" Emily asked. "If anything happens at all, they'll probably just think it's some great new earthquake ride or something."

"Not every kid is like you, Em." Nickie grinned, her foot bouncing in the air. "Some of them get freaked out when they don't know what's going on."

"Wait, are you talking about me as a kid or me now?"

"*But,*" Laura cut in, so she could finish her train of thought, "I got some pretty good advice yesterday I think we can use to our advantage. Or, at least, might make it harder for us to screw this up."

"Advice from who?" Nickie asked.

Laura dropped her head back against the ugly armchair. "From *whom*."

"Whatever. More wisdom from Winston?"

"No." Laura's gaze flickered toward Nickie, and a flush of color rose in her cheeks. "Not Winston."

"What other magicals do you work with who you can actually stand?" Emily chuckled.

"There's a…" Laura blinked, attempting not to give herself away, which was pretty much impossible. "There's a new professor starting this fall. He was moving into his office."

"Ooh. *He*." Emily wiggled her eyebrows. "Are you guys gonna go on some kinda totally nerdy archaeology date or something?"

"No dates." Laura shot her a scathing glance. "And he's a physics professor who got an office down the hall from mine because the Natural Sciences Building is full. Okay?"

"Sounds like you sure are getting to know him quickly." Nickie snorted. "And you told him about our little Gorafrex hunter problem, so…is he a wizard?"

Laura pressed her lips together. "He's not a wizard."

"Oh." Emily's lower lip popped out in surprise. "Then what is he?"

Laura blinked. *There is no* way *I'm gonna tell them about meeting a part-Kashgar who magicked my desk drawer back together and, apparently, makes me blush. Why am I doing that?* "He's…a dwarf."

Emily barked out a laugh. "Well never mind, then." She turned toward Nickie and spread her arms. "Laura doesn't go out with short guys, remember? *Roger* has a better chance than a dwarf."

Nickie smirked and narrowed her eyes. "Hmm. Poor dwarf doesn't have a chance."

Laura stood. "So that's the end of this ridiculously useless conversation."

"What was his advice?" Nickie asked.

Her older sister froze and took a breath. "That this whole ship was designed to maintain balance, and whatever was built on top of the energy core—like a children's museum—was put there for a reason none of us will understand. So, most likely, if removing or destroying the core is gonna affect anything around it, the ship would likely do what it could to make sure nothing got tipped *too* far off balance. Which I'm hoping won't even be the case."

"Sounds like we already have the green light, then." Emily stood, jingling her keyring in her hand.

The teezler, who thought it was going to be crushed between the back of her shirt and the back of the armchair, leapt off Emily's back and onto the bowling bag before scrambling across the top and slipping through the tiny hole where it hadn't been zipped all the way shut.

"Not to do whatever we want." Laura pointed at her youngest sister. "And no...E-X-C-S—"

"No *Excsindo* spell. Yeah, I got it."

"Emily..." Nickie stood from the futon and shook her head.

"Oh. Right. Sorry." Emily mimed zipping her mouth and locking it, then dropped her shoulders and grinned. "So we're off?"

Laura glanced at all the paper butterflies the origami dragon had taken to chasing. They swarmed above the witches' heads toward a lava lamp on the shelf. "I think we should probably leave the Clubhouse first. I have no idea how our 'nobody but the Hadstrom sisters' magic is gonna mix with transport bubbles."

"Okay." Emily thumbed the coin on her keyring and vanished.

Laura rolled her eyes and looked at Nickie. "Does she seem unusually hyper to you?"

Nickie giggled. "That's just Emily when she's happy."

"Huh." The sisters pressed their thumbs into the thumbprints and left their secret Clubhouse.

"All right!" Emily clapped her hands together and rubbed them vigorously when her sisters appeared in front of her in the basement. "Bubble time."

Laura couldn't hide her chuckle, even when she shook her head. "This might be the trickiest part. Hopefully. We don't know what the energy core looks like or where it is exactly. Obviously, it's *under* the Thinkery, but that could be anywhere, so we need to be a-hundred-percent focused on where we're guiding the bubble. Got it?"

Her sisters nodded.

"Focus on finding the energy core under the Thinkery, because that's all we know. We just have to take it from there. *Conmeatus*." A translucent bubble grew on her flashing silver ring.

Emily snorted. "What? You're not gonna ask if we have any questions?"

Laura turned her lips to the side. "If you had any, you would've already asked." She stepped into the growing bubble. Her sisters followed, focused on finding the energy core.

CHAPTER FOURTEEN

The transport bubble popped, and the witches appeared in complete darkness.

"Ow. You're on my foot."

"Hey, you don't have to push."

"I do if I want your elbow out of my face. That is your elbow?"

One of them bumped against the wall and knocked something metal to the ground. The sisters froze, hoping no one heard them.

"*Lychnus*." Laura's silver ring flashed. A glowing white orb the size of a lightbulb illuminated in her hand.

"Nice." Emily disentangled herself from between her sisters and lifted her foot out of a cardboard box full of dirty rags. "Are we in, like, a maintenance closet?"

"That looks like a breaker box…" Nickie pointed at the panel on the wall beside them, and Laura drew the orb of light closer.

"I think so. Doesn't look like it's powering anything

though. And it's missing the…oh." Her foot kicked against the metal door one of them had knocked off the breaker box. "Okay we need to be careful. Keep the property damage to a minimum and all that."

"Except for the energy core." Emily grinned.

Laura frowned at her sister. "Yeah. Except for that." She turned around and muttered, *"Illucio."* The light in her palm lifted into the air and drifted a few feet up and in front of them.

"Let's go."

"Emily, be *careful.*"

"What?" Laughing softly, Emily spread her arms. "I'm pretty sure nobody is down here. Wherever here is. And your little light wouldn't steer us astray, right?" She turned to follow the light-bulb-sized orb floating overhead, almost skipping.

"Emily *just* being happy, huh?" Laura raised an eyebrow.

Nickie raised her eyebrows back. "Okay, maybe not *just.* Might be John."

"She said she barely knows him."

"Laura, that's not a prerequisite for getting' all giddy about someone," Nicki said. "You already know that, though, right?"

Laura blinked, then noticed the darkness fading as the light and Emily moved down the corridor. "Come on."

They caught up, following their sister down the passage to the right. There wasn't much to see but a few snapped, dead wires and cement walls. Emily reached out with her left hand to trail her fingers along the wall. The color of it didn't change under Laura's floating orb of light, but Emily could feel the difference. "Woah…"

"What's wrong?"

"Nothing's *wrong*, Laura. I just..." She tapped the wall again with her finger. "The wall changed."

"What do you mean 'the wall changed?'"

"It felt like cement. Now it feels like...I don't know. Metal. Check it out."

The orb of light retracted toward them once they stopped, and Laura joined Emily at the corridor wall. "You're right. It doesn't feel like cement."

"You know, if it actually *is* metal..." Nickie spread her arms. "Who here says it's pure iron?"

"That makes sense. Iron Gorafrex prison inside the ring of energy cores." Laura squinted down the corridor. "Does it look like this thing is curving to you guys?"

"Barely. Maybe a little."

Laura nodded. "Okay. Keep going. You might be right, Nickie. We might be pretty close."

After two minutes of walking, Laura's floating ball of light rose higher, leaving them in darkness. "Uh...wait a minute. *Reditus.*" The tiny orb pulled a U-turn and descended.

"*Lychnus.*" Emily's ring flashed copper, and she sent a second sphere ahead of them and to the right. "This thing goes on forever, doesn't it?"

"I don't think this is a hallway anymore." Nickie squinted into the fading darkness as the lights floated away, illuminating the large chamber ahead. "I can hardly see." She tossed her hand toward the darkness in frustration, and the black ring on her thumb flashed on its own. Her sisters' lights ballooned to twenty times their size, and the chamber around them illuminated fully.

"Man, that's bright." Emily shielded her eyes.

"You didn't mean to do that, did you?" Laura asked.

"I didn't even *think* about a spell." Nickie raised an eyebrow. "Have you noticed that the rings don't always need a spell for accidental magic?"

"Oh, yeah. I noticed." Laura gazed at the tall walls of the chamber, all smooth, dark, and a little shiny under the huge orbs of light. "I mean, spells and wands are necessary, right? Just slower. The rings were made for fighting a Gorafrex and locking it up. Not a lot of time for saying a spell or flicking a wand. Or trying to find it again if you drop it in a—"

"Uh…guys?" Emily's voice came from the left, sounding far away. "I think we found the energy core."

Her sisters turned and saw the massive cylinder rising from the chamber floor. It stood at least twenty feet tall and maybe half that in diameter, the cylinder made of something like glass and long metal, curving arms clamped to it every few feet.

"Em, I think you're right." Laura approached the cylinder to stand by her sister. "At least now we know what they look like."

"Yeah…" Nickie ran a hand through her hair. "I don't think it's gonna be as easy to dismantle as we thought."

"Only one way to find out." Laura pulled her keys from her back pocket, thumbed the coin, and disappeared.

Emily peered at Nickie. "I don't think we've ever done this much popping in and out of anywhere."

"You're obviously getting a kick out of it."

"I really am." They grabbed their keyrings and popped into the Clubhouse.

Laura already had the giant Velikan socket wrench resting over her shoulder. She raised an uncharacteristically mischievous eyebrow at her sisters. "It's like you're not even trying to keep up." She disappeared.

Emily barked out a laugh. "When she gets going, she really *gets going*." She slipped her fingers through the handles of the bowling bag.

Nickie picked up the sledgehammer and swung it up with a grunt to rest over her shoulder. "I hope she lets me get in at least one good swing with this thing. This is gonna be like…hitting a piñata for a noble cause."

Laughing, Emily pressed her thumb on her coin, and Nickie followed.

"Okay. Who wants to go first?" When both her younger sisters stared at her with open mouths, Laura rolled her eyes. "Come on. Of *course* I waited for you. This is part of the Hadstrom legacy for all three of us."

"Well, sort of." Emily set down the bowling bag and flexed her fingers. "I mean, we wouldn't really be down here if we'd stuck to the original legacy and kept the Gorafrex where it…" She glanced at Laura's darkening frown and shrugged. "I mean, yeah. We're doing this together. Legacy and everything."

Laura nodded at Nickie. "Wanna go first?"

"You don't have to ask me twice." Nickie walked a slow circle around the outside of the energy core, looking for weak spots or anything particularly fragile. For the most part, those were at the base of the core, where the glass-like cylinder emerged from a metal cradle that looked like the legs on a clawfoot bathtub.

Emily knelt by the bowing bag and unzipped it,

watching her sister so she didn't miss a thing. Her hands wrapped around the teal, fourteen-pound bowling ball. The minute she lifted it and stood, the stowaway teezler scrambled unseen up the side of the bag, leapt out, and disappeared behind the energy core.

"All right. This is gonna be fun." Nickie dropped the sledgehammer to the chamber floor, tightened her grip, and swung it back in a wide arc. She brought the head down on both the bottom of the glass cylinder and the metal cradle holding it. An ear-splitting crack and a loud, piercing ring echoed upon impact.

Laura took a few steps back. "Jeeze."

"I felt that in my teeth." Emily stuck a finger in her ear and wiggled it around, flexing her jaw.

Nickie grinned. "I've always wanted to hit something with a sledgehammer." She pulled it back, swung it up, and brought it down hard. Something sparked, and Laura grimaced. The middle Hadstrom sister gave her hammer one good swing before stepping back. "Man. I guess at least it's good practice."

Laura balked. "For what?"

"You know, when I get really big. Like bigger-than-Austin famous. It probably won't happen, but if the mood ever strikes one day, at least I'll know I can smash a guitar."

Emily snorted, then burst out laughing as she hefted the weight of the bowling ball in her hands.

"Nickie." Laura stared at her with wide eyes. "You wouldn't actually *do* that, would you?"

"Really?"

"Yeah, really. It's a completely useless, wasteful, violent—"

"Laura, of *course* I would never do it." Nickie propped both hands up on the end of the sledgehammer's handle and cocked her head in surprise. "I'm kinda attached to my guitar being...attached."

Emily laughed. "No, she'd just break it Stevie Ray Vaughan style and play the crap out of it until it falls apart. You're close, Nickie. You should start bringing a backup with you."

Nickie grinned and pointed at Emily with a wink. "There you go."

"That actually happens?" Laura's head turned side to side as she glanced between her sisters.

"Oh, yeah." Emily stuck her thumb and two middle fingers into the bowling ball's worn inserts. "Google it." She took a few steps back, swung the bowling ball behind her, and burst out laughing. "Sorry. Sorry. If I throw it like that, this is gonna turn into the Energy Core Bowling Alley."

Nickie snorted, and Laura rolled her eyes.

"Lemme just...I'm gonna figure this out. Hold on." Emily lifted the ball in front of her chest, then closed her eyes and thought of how she could do the most damage. Then, she nodded, swung the ball back, and launched it at the energy core's column of glass. The copper ring on her thumb flashed. "*Impe*—what?"

The teal bowling ball burst with a bright-orange light and, with a crack like thunder, it shot like a cannonball from Emily's hands. The ball struck the glass-which-wasn't-quite-glass with a deafening crack. Sparks flew and ripples of bright-green magic scattered across the cylinder like an electrical current. The ball remained where it was, wedged halfway through the bowling-ball-sized hole it had made in the cylinder.

CHAPTER FIFTEEN

Emily gazed at the bowling ball and jumped back, shielding her eyes as another burst of sparks rained down. "Note to self. Never try that at an actual bowling alley."

Nickie threw her head back and roared with laughter.

Laura craned her neck to stare at the stuck bowling ball and giggled. "You know, I…I think that's probably the best place for it, Em. And if Dad ever asks…" A sharp, surprised laugh escaped her. "I'll tell him…that it's…" She burst out laughing.

Emily folded her arms, grinning. "That it's what?"

"That it's part of the legacy!" Laura tried to suppress her laughter.

Emily glanced up at the teal ball. "I think he might actually appreciate that. Woah." She huffed out a breath and couldn't decide whether to laugh or cry out. "I just had the best idea, like, ever."

Nickie gestured toward her from the top of the sledgehammer handle. "Care to enlighten us?"

"Not yet. I still have to—" The youngest witch stopped when a small white ball dropped right down the middle of the clear cylinder and disappeared at the bottom beneath the metal base. "What the heck was that?"

Laura wiped a few tears from her eyes. "What?"

"I just saw…" Emily stepped toward the energy core to look at the bottom. The minute she pressed her fingers against the glass-like wall, green sparks rose to meet her hands with a buzz and snap. "Ow." She jerked her hands back, shook them out, and looked inside again. unable to see anything. "I swear something dropped down the middle of this thing. It was white. Maybe round. I dunno." Stepping back to peer at the ceiling, she reached out her hand and waved it toward the top of the energy core. Her copper ring flashed, and the huge ball of light she'd summoned drifted across the ceiling, lighting the top of the core attached there just like it was attached to the floor.

"Maybe a few parts are coming loose?" Nickie stared at the ceiling and shrugged.

"You realize you didn't cast a spell or anything, right?" Laura watched Emily studying the ceiling.

The youngest lowered her head and turned to Laura with a grin. "Hey…you're right. Like it read my mind."

"More like you're a Hadstrom, and that's what it's supposed to do. I think." Laura returned the grin and glanced at her own ring. "At least this part of the legacy isn't the worst-case scenario."

"Wait, do you hear that?" Nickie raised a hand to shush them. "Listen…"

They heard a crunch and a metallic groan, followed by a few muffled thumps.

"Did that sound like a squeak to you guys?" Emily asked.

Laura stepped toward the energy core, bending a little to check it out. "I don't know, but it—jeeze!" A flare of green sparks erupted from the center of the clear cylinder, spraying in all directions like a firehose without anyone holding it steady. More metal groaned and squealed, the sparks lit up in bright, banging flashes, and the cylinder trembled.

"Laura, I thought you said the big ship was supposed to balance out whatever we did in here." Emily stepped away from the core, but was powerless to look at anything else.

"That was just a guess. And it wasn't even *my* guess."

The column cracked and sparked, making them all jump. A second later, flying green sparks of magical technology diminished, replaced by a column of steam hissing from somewhere at the base.

"Um…not that I'm complaining or anything." Nickie cocked her head. "But if this thing is broken, that's a little anticlimactic, right?"

Neither of her sisters said a word, instead waiting for the final explosion or tremble in the ground or whatever awful thing would signal their success.

"Think it's a good time to leave?" Emily asked.

A loud, desperate-sounding squeak rose from the base of the column. Something banged around in there with a sound like a mouse's claws scrabbling inside a metal sink. A puff of steam spurted from one of the arches between the energy core's many claw-like feet. A small white ball of fluff pushed its way out, swaying a little. The escaped teezler let out a high-pitched cough, which might or might not have triggered the static green burst along its fur.

Emily almost choked on her laughter and surprise.

"Harmless, huh?" Laura folded her arms.

"Well *yeah*. At least to us." With a chuckle, Emily crouched into a squat and grinned at the deviant teezler. "How'd you get here, huh? Did you go in there and break everything?"

The creature ruffled its fur, blinked wide round eyes at her, and nodded with another little squeak. It glanced at Laura and shrank toward the floor.

"Looks like it did a pretty good job, too." Nickie nodded at the energy core. "I'd say the thing's pretty broken."

Right on cue, another burst of green sparks flared inside the clear cylinder.

The teezler jumped, spun around, and chattered angrily at the metal base before sheepishly eyeing Emily. "Did you wreak massive destruction in there, little fella?"

The tiny creature nodded vigorously. Laughing, she scooped it up and squinted. "How did you even—" The teezler flung a tiny, fluffy arm toward the bowling bag. "Ooh. Very clever. Don't do it again."

Laura puffed out a sigh. "That's kind of a bummer..."

"What?" Nickie smirked and hefted the sledgehammer over her shoulder again. "Since when do you say bummer?"

"I don't know. I just..." Laura shook her head and slipped the massive socket wrench off her shoulder. "I let you guys go first 'cause I was trying to make up for sneaking out to find the Engineer and..." She shrugged.

"Well that was nice of you."

"Yeah, but I..." Laura blinked, confused by her own

reaction. She glanced at the energy core as she passed it and strode toward her sisters. "I *really* wanted to hit something." Like a little kid who just got told to quit running in the house and go play somewhere else, Laura smacked the Velikan socket wrench against the dismantled energy core.

Laura's ring flashed silver, and the wrench sent a cracking jolt of destructive magic through the cylinder. It launched the wrench out of her hand and sent it hurtling across the chamber toward her sisters. Shouting in surprise, Emily ducked, and Nickie leapt to the side.

Next to Laura, the energy core shuddered with a series of blazing silver and electric-blue flashes, and a wave of explosions boomed all the way up the clear tube. Laura reeled backward and gawped at the rising devastation. A massive, jagged crack split the metal and the glass-like material of the cylinder all the way around at the base. The chamber groaned and shuddered, and the energy core split from its cradle on the ceiling. It began a slow, terrifying collapse like a felled tree.

"Okay, *now* would be the time to get outta here," Emily shouted. Without knowing why, she snatched up the empty bowling bag as the teezler jumped inside it. Laura and Nickie were already running down the corridor the way they'd come, and Emily pushed herself to keep up.

The falling energy core groaned behind them, lighting up the passageway with green and blue sparks. Hissing steam echoed from everywhere until it was so loud, it hurt.

"*Conmeatus!*" Laura shouted. A shimmering transport bubble burst from her ring and drifted in front of them as it grew. "Come on. Hurry up!" She stepped into the bubble and waved Nickie forward. Nickie dropped the sledge-hammer and picked up the pace.

The minute she reached the bubble, she whirled around to see Emily sprinting down the corridor, arms pumping, bag tucked beneath one, as the energy-core chamber exploded in brilliant hues of blue and green and an orange she hoped wasn't fire. "Emily, come on!"

The hallway trembled and shuddered, knocking Emily off balance. Those few seconds she lost were just enough. She reached for Nickie's outstretched fingers, but the transport bubble disappeared, taking her sisters with it.

CHAPTER SIXTEEN

The bubble popped and dropped Nickie and Laura in the middle of the foyer.

"No!" Nickie whirled around, blinking, and ran a hand through her hair. "Where is she?"

"Oh, my god." Laura blinked, the image of her little sister chased down by a magical explosion burned into her brain.

"Laura! We have to do something."

"She's…she'll be here."

"She's *not* here." Nickie groaned. She spun in a circle. "We have to go back. What if she's stuck? What if she's unconscious? What if—screw it." She lifted her hand and took a breath. "*Conmea—*"

Laura grabbed her sister's wrist. "Wait. There might not be anything left to transport *to*. What if the next bubble drops us into that explosion, huh? Just think about it."

"Why don't *you* think about what's gonna happen when Emily doesn't show up!" Nickie opened her mouth to cast the spell, but something thumped onto the huge staircase behind them.

Six more bumps later, Emily stopped tumbling down the stairs. She hit the landing upside-down, on her back, her legs stretched out on the stairs above her and her shoulder and head shoved against the wall. "Ow…"

"Oh, my god! Em…" Nickie dropped at the base of the stairs and helped Emily sit up. Groaning, Emily got her feet the rest of the way down the stairs, patted Nickie's shoulder, and rubbed her head. "Are you crazy? You stopped to pick up a stupid *bowling bag*."

"Oh, yeah." Emily shifted to get the corner of the bag out from under her, then held it up. "Success."

"Success?"

"Nickie, you're sounding a lot like Laura right now, and there's only one Laura, thank god." Emily grinned up at their oldest sister and paused. "Hey, I'm okay. Promise."

Laura stood there in the hallway, both hands clamped over her mouth as she stared at Nickie and Emily on the floor. "Yeah." It came out muffled and squeaky, and she dropped her hands. "Yeah, Em. You're okay."

Nickie shot her a furious glance, and Laura couldn't ignore the swell of guilt building in her gut. "You cast a bubble, right?"

Emily shot her two thumbs-up. "Best way to travel." She glanced back and forth between her sisters and frowned. "You guys didn't think I could do it on my own, did you?"

"We didn't know what to think," Nickie said softly.

"How 'bout giving me a little credit here, huh?" Emily picked herself up off the floor, grimacing at the soreness in her neck. "I know I'm still the baby. I'll always be the youngest, and I get that, but I'm not actually *a baby*. I can handle spells and bubbles and running from explosions just as well as you can."

Nickie dropped her head back against the wall and straightened her legs out on the floor. "We know you can, Em. But you stopped. To pick up a *bag*."

"Yeah? Well this *bag*"—Emily swung it out and tossed it onto the foyer floor—"was a custom order, right? Dad printed 'Magic 14' on there just for you, Laura. I don't know who else would even be stupid enough to go down there besides the Gorafrex, but even if it's just that *thing*, it'd pretty dumb to leave something lying around that points back to us. You know, just trying to be smart. Good to know how low your expectations are." Without looking at either of them, Emily stormed past them and out the front door.

"Come on, Em." Nickie spread her arms. "Where are you going?"

"Out," she called over her shoulder.

Laura opened her mouth to say something—anything—to get her sister to stay. Instead, what came out was, "In this heat?"

The door slammed shut. Emily was gone.

"Really, Laura?"

"What?"

"In this heat?"

Laura blinked and gestured toward the door. "Heat-stroke's a thing. What should I have said?"

"I don't know." Nickie shook her head, stood, and ran a hand through her hair. "I need some water or something."

She headed off through the dining room and into the kitchen.

Laura glanced at the bowling bag on the floor. A white, fluffy head poked out of one corner. "Oh, no. You stay in there."

The teezler blinked when she pointed at it. "You were helpful, to be honest, but that doesn't mean you get to stay out of your pen. Come on." She bent to pick up the bag, and the furry creature chattered away at her. "Yeah, yeah. Congratulations." Laura frowned down at the thing, then dropped her frown and sighed at the teezler. "You might have changed my mind about you little guys though."

The rogue teezler received a boisterous welcome from its fellow creatures upon being returned to its pen. Laura shut the door and propped the box up against the tote, then went upstairs and found Nickie in the kitchen at the table, phone in hand, watching a news clip.

"What's that?" Laura went to the sink to get a glass of water.

"Breaking news." Nickie turned up the volume and flipped the phone around so Laura could see. "Earthquake in northeast Austin. They're calling it a three-point-four on the Richter scale."

"Ugh. The Thinkery?"

"Yep."

Laura blinked, took a long drink of water, and sighed. "Just tell me…was anyone hurt?"

Her sister smiled and closed the news clip. "Nope. Couple of toddlers fell over, but that's what they do." She shrugged. "I guess that means we—" Her phone dinged, followed by four more in quick succession. "Crap. Chuck's been trying to get ahold of me. Why didn't I get these?"

Laura pulled out a chair and joined her at the table. "Maybe we were just *really* far underground. It's not like we climbed down a ladder or anything."

"Right." Nickie read through all the texts and sighed. "I need to call him." She pressed the call button. After the first ring, their front door swung open with a little creak.

"Hello?"

Nickie stared at her phone, ended the call, and turned toward the dining room. "We're in the kitchen." She shot Laura a surprised grimace.

"Babe, what happened to your phone? I've been texting all morning."

"Yeah, sorry. We didn't have reception."

Laura bit back a laugh, which was harder to do when Nickie shot her a warning glance.

"Where did you guys—woah." Chuck stopped at the long dining room table the Hadstrom sisters never used. Except now, it held all the iron weapons Laura's ring had forged almost a week ago. "You guys takin' these to the Renaissance Festival or somethin'?"

Nickie's eyes widened, and she and Laura stood and joined him in the dining room. "Oh. *Those.*" Nickie stopped on the other side of the table, folded her arms, and nodded at the array of oddities—an iron lance longer than the table and two random iron spheres that released some kind of thin iron thread at the push of a button. *And only Emily can touch them, apparently. Good thing we left the daggers in our cars...* "We just found these today." She glanced at Laura and nodded.

"Huh." Chuck rubbed his chin and studied the items. "You guys went looking for a spear and a couple of... what? Metal balls? In an antique shop without reception?"

Nickie glanced at Laura and nodded. "Yep..."

Laura grinned at Chuck. "Special kind of antique shop. They carry really old weapons hardly anybody wants. We went through a lot of junk."

"A *lot* of junk." They both nodded at him.

"Huh." Chuck laughed. "You know, that's not even the weirdest thing you guys have done, so okay." He leaned over the table for a closer look at one of the iron orbs. "This thing doesn't look very old, though. I mean, is that some kinda button..." He lifted the iron orb in both hands and tossed it.

"Chuck, it's not a toy," Laura said.

"Uh...babe? Maybe you should put that down."

"Woah, it's pretty heavy. Have you guys figured out what this thing does?" His finger moved toward the circular button on the top of the orb.

"No!" Laura shouted. She rushed around the table and plucked the sphere from him. Chuck blinked at her in surprise. "Come on, Chuck. We *just* got them, and they're important for this...project I've got going on. I just don't want to mess with them yet, 'kay?"

His hands, now empty, hadn't moved. "Uh..." Chuck blinked and glanced at Nickie, who shrugged. "Right. Sorry."

"Totally fine." Laura cocked her head and placed the

iron orb back down on the table. "So what're you doing here?"

"Oh. I mean, I knew you guys were going out to look for stuff. Didn't know you were looking for weapons…"

"You knew, huh?" Laura shot Nickie an accusatory glance, and her sister shook her head before smiling at Chuck again.

"Yeah, Nickie told me yesterday. I'm not trying to interrupt anything, if you guys are still doing your thing, or whatever. Babe, did you get my texts?"

"Literally right before you walked in the door. Sorry."

"Did you *read* them?"

"Yeah." When Chuck widened his eyes, Nickie jolted a little and blinked. "Oh, yeah. Right. Dave wants to have a meeting."

"He sure does." A tiny frown flickered over Chuck's brows as he studied her. "So I was thinking maybe we could—"

The front door burst open. Emily continued her determined stomping and walked into the dining room. She stopped. "Oh. Hey, what's up, Chuck?" She snorted and shook her head. "Get it? Upchuck?" She walked around him, leaned forward, and snatched the metal orb from the table.

"Hey, Em…" Chuck glanced at her, then watched her walk back toward the foyer, orb in hand. "Where, uh, you goin' with that thing?"

"To practice in the basement." Emily stopped short in the foyer, blinked, and shook her head. "Nope. Not the basement." She took the stairs two at a time.

Chuck glanced at Nickie with a raised eyebrow. "I

thought you guys didn't have a basement."

"That's why I can't practice there," Emily called from the top of the stairs. "Catcha later." Her bedroom door opened and closed, and everyone in the dining room stared at one another a few seconds.

"Practicing *what?*" Chuck laughed in an awkward way.

"Oh. She thinks these things are some kinda medieval bowling ball or something." Laura turned toward Nickie and opened her mouth.

Nickie shook her head the tiniest bit, then, "Come sit, babe." She nodded toward the living room across the foyer. "I wanna know what Dave has to say."

"You sure? I mean, if you guys aren't done, I can—"

"Yep. I'm sure. Let's go." She walked around the table and grabbed his hand, leading him into the living room.

"Yep, all good," Laura called behind them. "I have a few things to go look up, so I'll just…" She sighed and turned back to the kitchen. "Awesome. One energy core activated, one destroyed, ten more to go."

Laura slumped into her chair at the kitchen table and drank the rest of her water. "And that *thing* is still out there. Definitely still inside a human host. Definitely getting ready to kill another witch. Or a wizard. And we have no idea where to look for it or how to find it unless Nickie plays Dad's lullaby again and brings it right—"

Her phone buzzed in her back pocket and nearly made her fall out of the chair. She didn't recognize the number. *But it's not like I can afford to avoid potentially important phone calls.* Her finger came down on the green button to accept the call. "Dr. Laura Hadstrom."

"Hi, Professor."

CHAPTER SEVENTEEN

Laura pulled the phone away from her ear to double-check the number, then brought it back up. "Um… who's calling?"

"It's me, Laura. Your less-than-completely human neighbor from down the hall."

She blinked, and the pause obviously got to him.

"O-on campus, I mean." Nathan chuckled on the other end of the line. "I have no idea where you live. Promise."

"Nathan…" Laura caught herself, remembering Nickie and Chuck in the other room. "How did you get my personal number?"

"You answer your personal phone with *Dr. Laura Hadstrom?*"

"You know what I mean."

"Yeah." He chuckled. "Yeah, I do. There's a staff contact list in the main office. No snooping, I swear. Okay, a little snooping. It was in the main office in the director's office."

Unbelievable. Laura shook her head and leaned back in

the chair. "And why are you calling me at three o'clock in the afternoon on a Saturday?"

"Well…" This time, his laugh sounded less confident. "I wanted to invite you to a party, actually."

"A what?"

"A party. You know, where people get together outside working hours? Have a few drinks, Some friendly conversation—"

"I know what a party is." She forced herself to lower her voice. "I just don't know why you're asking *me* to go with *you*."

"You don't?"

"No. I don't." *Especially because he's part Kashgar, and that is more trouble for me than I can handle.*

"Huh. You don't know why I…" Nathan cleared his throat. "Well, if I'm being honest, I enjoyed meeting you yesterday. I think you're fun, and I'm into the fact that you're an archaeologist. I don't know any archaeologists, technically speaking, so I was hoping you'd say, 'Screw it. Why not? I'll give it a shot.'"

"You *what*?"

"Okay…" He exhaled into the phone, a much smaller laugh coming through. "Is this a thing you do, where you ask someone to repeat everything they say? Or is your plan to make me feel like a rambling idiot until I just give up? 'Cause it could go either way at this point. I'm, uh, fine with whatever happens, but I just…can't tell."

Despite her reservations, a smile tugged at the corners of her mouth. *That was refreshingly honest. I actually think he's embarrassed.*

"Are…you still there?"

"What?" She blinked. "I mean, yes. Yeah, I'm still here."

"Well *that's* a relief. So…would you like to come to this party with me?"

Laura confused herself by not saying no right off the bat. "When is it?"

"Tomorrow. I know. Why have a party on a Sunday night, right? It's sort of a 'Welcome to Austin' kind of party."

"For whom?"

"Uh…for me?" He puffed out a clipped, hesitant laugh. "I mean, it's summer break, right? Good news for us. We don't have class on Monday. *Yay…*"

Laura laughed. "True."

"I gotta say I'm really glad you didn't ask me to repeat *that* part."

"Yeah, that's just…" *A way of hiding my cluelessness.* She shook her head. "I'll think about it, Nathan. Okay?"

"Yeah. Sure. Sounds great. Just lemme know before, say, four o'clock tomorrow? At least then I can scrub off my disappointed face before I arrive at my own party."

"Are you playing the guilt-trip card with someone you just met?"

He snorted. "Is it working?"

Laura's smile grew, and she rolled her eyes. "I'll think about it. And I'll let you know before four o'clock tomorrow."

"Perfect. Is that your final answer?"

"Goodbye, Nathan."

"Yep. Bye."

He ended the call first, and an image popped into her head of him stabbing at the phone, tossing it aside, and falling over somewhere. "That conversation couldn't have gone the way either one of us wanted it to." Laura stared at her phone. "I'm actually considering going to a party with a Kashgar?"

She spent the next half hour split between wondering how much damage another 'earthquake' caused by them destroying another energy core would mess with essential functions at the airport, and also what in the world she was going to decide about Nathan's party. The only thing that drew her out of both unsolved mysteries was Chuck peeking his head around the corner and into the dining room.

"Bye, Laura." He stretched his hand out and wiggled his fingers at her.

Blinking, she looked at him before realizing he was talking to her. "Oh. Bye, Chuck. Good to see ya."

"Yeah, you too." He glanced at the iron orb still on the table and the lance. "Good luck with your project and all the...antiques."

"Right. Thanks." She waved and offered a quick smile.

Nickie went with Chuck to the foyer, kissed him good-bye, and waited until he'd gone down the steps on the hill before shutting the front door. She turned and thumped her back against it with a groan. "This keeps getting worse."

"What does?" Laura lifted her empty glass and considered refilling it. *Why am I considering it?*

"Chuck. This whole Gorafrex thing. Ripping up energy cores." Nickie dragged her hands down her cheeks, shook her head, and headed into the dining room. "I *hate* having to lie to him."

"You've been doing it for a few years already. It's bound to just keep getting worse."

"Oh, that's great, Laura. No, it's not *bound* to do anything." Nickie gripped the back of a chair and dropped her head with a sigh. "I can't ever tell him about us. That I'm a witch. That magic is a thing or we're all just floating around and around on a planet-shaped vessel that wasn't supposed to be here in the first place. And that was fine. I could handle that. But now I literally have to lie to him about everything that doesn't directly involve him, and it's only been a week, and I think it's killing me."

Laura settled on not refilling her water and pushed the glass across the table. "I wish I had something to tell you to make you feel better."

"I know."

"I'm sorry."

"I know that too."

Closing her eyes, Laura stuck her cell phone into her back pocket. "But we can do this, Nickie. The three of us. We proved that today." She headed into the dining room. "And maybe, when we get the Gorafrex—and we *will* —maybe you can go back to only lying to Chuck about the little things."

Nickie snorted. "The little things, huh?"

"In comparison." Laura smirked.

"Yeah. Small lies would be nice about now."

They stood in silence for a few seconds, then Laura looked up from the glinting iron lance on the table. "So, you told him we were going out for a *project* today?"

Nickie puffed out a breath. "Yeah. I said you had something to do for work and wanted Emily and me to help you look for some kinda artifact. So good job, I guess, on explaining these things." She gestured toward the two weapons. "Actually, he asked if he could come with us."

"What did you tell him?"

"That you'd planned this whole thing for us, and it was supposed to just be a sister thing. To help you with your *project.*"

"That's…incredibly accurate, actually."

"Yeah, well, the best lies are hidden in the truth, I guess."

The walls suddenly groaned and rumbled. Just off the dining room, the foyer morphed in its magically-induced rearrangement of walls, floors, and ceiling. A wall folded into existence where the entryway normally was, and the repetitive clack of wood hitting wood echoed through the house as the main staircase to the second floor folded in on itself. Just as quickly, the walls and corners blocking them from the foyer shifted back into place, disappearing into the floor and sliding in ten different ways.

The door that existed where the staircase usually was burst open. Emily darted out of the magical door from the basement, the iron orb clenched in both hands, and stumbled into the dining room with her sisters. "You guys. I think—"

The house rumbled, clacked, thumped, and shifted, drowning out every other sound. Emily rolled her eyes and waited, using the few seconds to catch her breath before she started over.

"I think I figured out what these weird metal spheres are for! Wait, Chuck left, right?"

"Just now, yeah." Nickie raised an eyebrow.

"Okay, good. So, remember what happened with the bowling ball and—"

"Wait." Laura frowned and glanced into the foyer. "I thought you took that thing up to your room."

"I did. So the—"

"Then how did you just come from the basement?"

Emily grinned. "Transport bubbles are pretty freakin' awesome, right? Any more questions before I try one more time to tell you something that's actually important?"

Her sisters glanced at each other and shook their heads.

"Okay. Thanks. What I've been *trying* to say is that I'm pretty sure Laura forged me some flying traps for the Gorafrex." Emily thrust the iron orb out with both hands and grinned.

CHAPTER EIGHTEEN

"Uh..." Nickie wrinkled her nose. "Say that again."

"Flying traps for the Gorafrex." Emily raised her eyebrows. "I'm thinking something like one of those super-old slingshots they had to swing around in circles before letting the rock fly. Or whatever. Only this one has a string attached, right? An *iron* string. Not sure how that's possible, but *hey*. It was made by a magical ring that's been around since everyone boarded this ship, so—"

"Okay, Em. Slow down a minute." Laura lifted her hands and closed her eyes. "Please."

"Why?" Emily laughed. "This isn't a super complicated thing. Think about it. What I did to the energy core with the bowling ball, right? Imagine the bowling ball with a little button on it and a weaponized bit of string that comes out." She nodded slowly, glancing back and forth between Laura and Nickie with wide, excited eyes.

"Oh..." Nickie cocked her head. "Plus that little magical power boost you gave it."

"Exactly. I mean, come on, I'm strong enough, but I

can't throw a bowling ball that hard. This thing isn't nearly as big, but I'm pretty sure it'll pack as much of a punch. Maybe more for the Gorafrex. Laura, what do you think?"

"I think…that's a *really* strange weapon for my ring to have randomly chosen to make."

Emily blinked. "Well, yeah. But at least I found *some* way to use it."

Laura cocked her head. "It's still super weird. Like, what are the odds any of us would've figured out the button or the string? Not to mention you think you can use it like a bowling ball to destroy energy cores and *maybe* the Gorafrex. And the part about that little iron string burning Nickie when she touched it. It'd probably burn me too."

"The odds?" Nickie chuckled. "I'd say a-hundred-percent, Laura. We're the only ones who can wear the rings now. Yours wouldn't have made these weapons for any other witch, right?"

"True." Laura shrugged, squinting at the orb in her sister's hand. "Okay, so we know pure iron's the only thing that'll weaken the Gorafrex enough for us to get it back in the prison. Also made of iron. Just like these weapons…" She moved her gaze to the other orb on the table and the lance. "What if my ring also chose *these* weapons to help us dismantle the cores?"

"Hey, *there's* an idea." Emily tossed the iron sphere in her hands. "All-purpose magical weapons."

"Wait, why did you call those things a net?" Nickie pointed at the orb.

Emily wiggled her eyebrows. "Wanna come see how it works?"

"Honestly, I'm both intrigued and terrified." Nickie laughed. "Yeah, I wanna see."

"Come on." The youngest Hadstrom sister stalked into the foyer, then called over her shoulder, "Laura, I was inviting you too, you know. You just might be impressed. Or struck with inspiration! Who knows?"

Laura blinked at the two weapons left on the table, then took a deep breath. "Yeah, okay." She stepped into the foyer just before the walls started shifting, sliding, folding, and dropping away everywhere but in the foyer itself.

The staircase squashed up like an accordion and disappeared into the floor. With a groan and a loud boom, the door to the Hadstrom sisters' basement appeared where the staircase had been. Emily leapt toward the door, jerked it open, and bounded down the stairs two at a time. Nickie laughed, and Laura walked slowly down behind them, wondering how in the world that orb in Emily's hand could be used as a weapon.

They went into the massive, sprawling basement, which could have been a concert hall if it had more auditorium seating than just six rows and less junk lining the walls. "Come *on*." Emily waved them forward and skipped to the far end of the basement, right between the rows of reclining chairs. She dropped the iron sphere onto the stage and jumped up after it.

Nickie laughed when she saw the mini training arena Emily had set up for herself on the stage. Laura stopped just behind the auditorium chairs and folded her arms. "What in the world, Emily?"

"Wow, you're really channeling Mom right now." Grinning, Emily gestured toward the setup she'd been using for target practice. "This guy's been a trooper."

"He doesn't really have a choice." Nickie chuckled and shook her head.

"Well, no. But I didn't want—"

"Where did you find a suit of armor, Em?" Laura raised an eyebrow.

"Just lying on the ground under that huge trunk over there." Emily pointed to the wall on Laura's right, where a huge trunk was propped open, a bunch of Victorian-era costumes spilling over the sides. "I bet whoever used that sword last also wore this armor. That'd be cool, right?"

"Not if you're using more family heirlooms and historical artifacts for target practice."

"Relax. The armor is fine. I found padding." Emily grinned.

Nickie cocked her head. "What are those? Rugs?"

"Curtains, actually. I think." Emily took her place on the right side of the stage and turned to face the standing suit of armor bundled up in thick, awkward rolls of dusty, red-velvet curtains. "Okay, check it out." She pressed the tiny circular button on the top of the orb, and a tiny compartment door swung open on the bottom. The thin, bright-silver string of iron dropped from the opening and dangled there. She took the string in her left hand, gripping it tight, and wound her arm back for a solid throw.

"You're way too close," Laura muttered.

Dropping into one of the chairs in the aisle, Nickie glared over her shoulder and shot Laura a warning glance. "Let her do her thing, huh?"

Laura rolled her eyes but settled for watching and

waiting.

Emily threw the iron orb. The moment it left her hand, the copper ring on her finger flashed. With a loud crack, the orb lit up and barreled at lightning speed toward the bundled suit of armor. Emily tugged the string with both hands, and the orb curved around the armor's left shoulder and back. In a matter of seconds, the ball had curved, lifted, and looped around the suit of armor in every direction, covering the shoulders, arms, hips, waist, back, and chest. The string drew taut, and when the orb completed a final swing, it knocked against the side of the helm with a hollow *clang*. The force of it sent the entire suit of armor off balance, almost in slow motion—the suit tipped backward and fell to the stage with a thump and a puff of dust.

"Woah!" Emily jerked forward across the stage, still holding the end of the string in both hands. When the dust settled, she turned toward her sisters in the audience and gave them an exaggerated bow.

Nickie burst into applause, the sound echoing in the giant basement. Laura's pursed lips twitched to the side, and she squinted at what was supposed to represent the fallen Gorafrex. "Just like tetherball. I'd say that's a good start."

"I know, right? See? Flying net!" Emily grinned and tugged on the iron string.

"You also just bashed the human host's head in with that thing."

"Laura…" Nickie shot her another exasperated glance.

"That's something we have to think about, right?" Laura gestured toward the stage. "I mean, the next time we see the Gorafrex, it's still gonna be inside a human. Sure, that human can't get hurt while the creature has control of his or her body, but whatever damage they sustain is gonna hit all at once the second the Gorafrex shrugs out of them like an old sweater. Do we really wanna add a head injury—and who knows what else that orb might do—to the list?"

"Laura, we *do* have healing spells," Nickie offered. "Remember when I burned my fingers on that string before? I'm pretty sure my ring tapped into the Peabrain magic I didn't know I could access. I was blowing healing bubbles all over the place. And they worked. Fingers good as new." She gestured toward the stage and the bundled-up suit of armor. "You don't honestly believe that after however long the Gorafrex has been inside a human, they won't already need a lot of healing anyway? If we're careful, and we time it right, none of that will matter."

"It's still *hurting* an innocent person."

"Okay." Emily nodded, still catching her breath after all the effort and concentration she'd put into the demonstration. "Sure, I still hafta work out a few kinks—and I won't stop practicing until I get it right—but I think this is one of the big things we were missing. Like, what if I'd known this was possible the other night when Nickie played at Tina's laundromat, huh? Who knows? I might've been able to tie the Gorafrex up with this thing and keep it from kidnapping that witch." She didn't have to say what each of the Hadstrom sisters were thinking; if they'd stopped the Gorafrex that night, it wouldn't have killed two people—one of them the witch—and using lifeforce magic to power one of the energy cores.

Laura blinked, eyed the mess of armor wrapped in curtains and iron string, and glanced at Emily. "If the

Gorafrex's host gets wrapped up like that, it should weaken it enough that the thing can't fly away again and go looking for someone else to use. It might actually…" She sighed. "Okay, fine. It's a decent plan."

"Yes!"

"But I'm *not* a fan of what that thing might do to the human host. You have to keep practicing." She pointed at Emily. "Find out how to control that thing to keep it from doing any real damage we might not be able to heal."

"Already on my schedule."

"And I really don't wanna hear about—"

"Em?" Nickie stood from the reclining stadium chair and peered at the stage. "What's on your hands?"

Emily glanced at her hands and opened them. The end of the iron string dropped to the stage with a metallic whisper. "Oh, wow." She chuckled. "Yeah, that's blood."

"*What?*" Laura hurried toward the stage and craned her neck up at her sister. "Let me see."

"Um…" Emily took a hesitant step sideways, trying to avoid the drops of blood she only now noticed trailing across the stage. Then she squatted in front of Laura and held out her hands, still wearing that goofy smile of disbelief. "Honestly, I didn't even feel it."

"Oh, my god." Laura held the backs of her sister's hands and studied the slashing lines across Emily's palms where the iron string had cut her deep. She shot out her hand toward the open trunk stuffed with clothing, and her silver legacy ring took it from there. A yellowed square of fabric shot from the trunk toward Laura's outstretched hand. She snatched it from the air and gently dabbed at the cuts on her sister's palms.

Emily looked at her. "Now who's ruining family heirlooms?"

Laura glanced up, then shook her head. "It's a handkerchief."

Nickie joined them and took a long breath. "Jeeze, Em. You're a mess."

"It's just blood." Emily shrugged. "Really, it doesn't even hurt."

"Well, it *will*. Just give it a min—" The words were strangled in Nickie's throat when a tiny stream of purple bubbles flew from her mouth. She clamped her jaw shut and scowled at the stream of healing magic heading for Emily's hands. "I really—" Another wave of bubbles sprang from her mouth, and Emily laughed at both her older sisters' irritation—and at the purple bubbles tickling her hands.

All three of them watched the deep cuts stitch together on Emily's skin until all that remained were the barest hint of lines across her palms. They were a darker pink than the rest of her hands and a little shiny with new skin, but they didn't even feel tight when she gave an experimental flex. "Thank you very much." Emily dipped her head matter-of-factly and grinned.

Nickie opened her mouth to test it. When no bubbles emerged, she scoffed. "I'm all for using Peabrain magic when it's the right fit. Which that obviously was. But come on? My mouth?"

Emily shrugged. "Maybe it's to keep the healer from annoying and berating the person needing the healing. A quick recovery needs a lot of peace and quiet, right?"

For a few seconds, her sisters stared in mute surprise.

Laura giggled, and when she couldn't hold it back, it grew into uncontrollable laughter that overwhelmed her until she had to brace against the edge of the stage. "You... you..." Without lifting her head, she jerked a finger toward Nickie and kept laughing.

Nickie squinted and folded her arms. "Very funny."

Emily laughed and nodded at Laura. "The very serious professor seems to think so."

Laura took a few breaths and blew them out. Still chuckling, she wiped her eyes and lifted her head. "Is that what you call me? The very serious professor?"

Humming and glancing at the high basement ceiling, Emily pretended to think about it. "Only your good days."

Laura found this only slightly less funny than the remark about healing, but she pulled herself together. "Do I wanna know what you call me on bad days?"

"Probably not."

Nickie snorted, and Laura dipped her head in acknowledgment. "Fair enough."

Emily spread her arms and glanced at the stage floor and behind her. "Man, that was a lot of blood." She plucked the stained handkerchief from Laura's hand and got to work cleaning it all up. "That's one of the kinks, I think. Figuring out how to not slice up my hands every time I get jerked around by that thing."

"Yeah, I doubt the Gorafrex inside a human's body is gonna stay as still as that armor," Nickie said.

"I *did* have an incredibly willing volunteer, didn't I?" Emily laughed as she wiped more blood spatter off the stage.

CHAPTER NINETEEN

Nickie sprawled across the length of the couch in the living room, a foot dangling over the cushion and onto the floor. She finger-picked a simple tune on her acoustic, enjoying the sunlight spilling through the old house's huge bay windows, yet the sun never made the room uncomfortably hot. "Magical AC. I am so down."

She played a little more and caught the scent of the spatchcock chicken in the oven—lemon and garlic and olive oil. "So really, Em," she called through the mudroom without getting up. "You spend as much time as you do in the kitchen at Meadowlark, and you still wanna cook for us on your day off?"

Emily bent down beside the stove to sneak a glance at the pan of chicken inside. "Technically, it's not my day off. I told you guys I switched around my shifts for what I *thought* was gonna be the three of us going to see the Engineer today…"

"I get it, okay?" Laura sat at the kitchen table, reading through the Peabrain spellbook from her former colleague admirer. "I won't go off on my own anymore when we plan to do something together." She tilted her head at the book. *Doesn't mean I can't ever go off on my own.* "Hey, but it's a good thing I moved the timeline up, right? You had today off to come bash up that energy core with us *and* figure out how to use that metal yo-yo."

Emily straightened and slapped a hand down on the counter. "In no way whatsoever should we call that thing a yo-yo."

Looking up from the spellbook, Laura raised an eyebrow. "Okay, then. What do *you* call it?"

"I…am still working on that part." The Meadowlark Tavern's young commis chef turned around and grabbed three plates from the cabinet. "Oh, *Nickie*…come and get it…"

The soft guitar music in the other room stopped.

Laura chuckled. "I get dinner, too, right?"

"Yeah, but you're sitting right behind me. Come on." On went the oven mitt, and she pulled the pan of chicken out and set it on top of the stove.

"Wow." Laura closed the spellbook. "That smells amazing."

"I know. Oh. Almost forgot." Emily took the lid off the sauté pan, set it aside, then took two steps sideways and tugged on the long, magical conveyor belt that was her spice rack. The various bottles, jars, and sealed packages flipped past her like a larger-than-life rolodex. When the spice jars reached the end of the counter, they disappeared into the wall and didn't stop until Emily pointed. She grabbed an unlabeled jar of red powder with flecks of purple in it and unscrewed the lid.

"What's that?" Laura asked.

"Secret ingredient."

"What? Come on, just tell me."

"It's magic, Laura, okay?" Emily tapped a bit into the sauté pan, then dusted it over the chicken. "That's like asking a magician how they do their tricks before you even watch the show."

"Okay, real magic is actually a thing though. It's a little weird comparing your cooking to what magicians do."

Nickie stepped into the kitchen and ran a hand through her dark-brown hair. "You know, I bet you anything there's a wizard or witch out there who performs as a stage magician and hopes nobody notices the difference."

Laura frowned. "Why would anyone wanna do that?"

"Easiest job in the world." Nickie shrugged and went to pull them each a set of silverware from the drawer.

"Except your entire career is based on a lie about not lying about magic."

Emily chuckled. "Say what?"

"Everyone knows magicians do tricks. Even if they can't explain how those tricks are performed, it's pretty cut and dried across the board; there is no actual *magic* in those performances. A magical trying to pull off being a magician with *fake magic* is gonna spend their entire career knowing everyone thinks it's fake when it's actually real."

Nickie blinked. "That made me a little dizzy."

Laura scoffed. "You'd have to pretend to be a fake, and you could never claim credit for knowing real magic."

"*Oh...*" Emily nodded as she plated up three equal portions of chicken and sauce and a few slices of lemon. "That makes sense coming from you."

"What's that supposed to mean?"

"Laura, not everybody's as dedicated as you are to following the rules," she turned and made air quotes, "and earning accolades and being credited for things they're passionate about."

Nickie glanced at the sautéed veggies as Emily scooped them onto their plates, then brought the silverware to the table. "Some people like to take the easy road. If they're good at being a magician 'cause they can actually *use* magic for real, and they're getting paid for it, why worry about what the rest of the world thinks? It's not like this hypothetical magician wouldn't be able to use magic at all if they had to pick a different job."

The oldest Hadstrom sister reclined and shook her head. "I still think it's a cheap way to make a living."

Emily stepped toward the table with two plates balanced on one arm and the third in her other hand. "Okay, so explain what *we* do, then."

"What? We're not talking about us."

"Well, we kind of are, though." Nickie reached up to take the first plate from Emily with a grin. "How are any of us any different than this hypothetical magical who decided to become a performing magician?"

"I mean, none of us are magicians."

Emily snorted, set the other two plates on the table, and sat. "No, but it's definitely the same thing. You're an archaeologist first. Yeah, and a professor—still totally weird to say—but you do what you do for a reason. You've always had creepy skills with magical artifacts, right? I dunno, maybe your magic blends with theirs better than most or whatever. But you used that to pick your job."

"My *career*." Laura blinked and picked up her fork. "And I went to college and studied and worked my butt off for my PhD like everybody else who has one. I can prove it."

"Yeah, we know." Nickie set to work cutting up her chicken. "You've probably got an entire wall with all your degrees and awards and certifications framed perfectly and hung all in a straight, neat little row for everyone to see."

Laura paused and stared at her, lips pressed together. "Have you been in my room?"

"No, Laura. I have no desire to spend hours and hours trying to undo your wards so I can sneak around and read your archaeology professor journal."

Emily choked on her first bite and tried to hide her laughter with a quick series of coughs. "Yeah, maybe Laura's not such a great example for making my point."

"So then let's talk about what I do." Nickie tipped her fork toward Emily, chewing slowly. "This is amazing. What are these?"

"Kale, shaved carrots, thinly sliced leeks…"

"And a *secret* ingredient." Laura exaggerated the mystery of it with wide eyes, leaning over the table toward them.

"Nope. I'm not telling. Nickie, please continue proving my point."

"Right." Nickie grinned and kept eating. "I'm a full-time musician. Okay, maybe not full-time yet, but I get paid pretty well for gigs, and that holds me over until the next one. Or until a big break. *Oh*, which might actually be happening soon, by the way."

"Really?" Laura swallowed her mouthful. "What's going on?"

"I'll tell you that in a sec. What I was gonna say is that

being a musician is my job. Yes. And I absolutely love it, hands down."

"Good. You should." Laura nodded. "You're ridiculously talented, and everybody sees it."

"Right, but that's what I'm trying to get at here. *I* don't even know how much of that *talent* is talent in the traditional sense, or how much of it comes from my own magic. I just don't know. Only that it *makes* me a better musician."

"Like whether you'd still be the new Queen of Blues without your magic or just some hack plucking at a couple strings." Emily nodded.

"Well…yeah. I guess." Nickie laughed. "If we're gonna be that blunt about it."

"But Nickie's not using her magic to make people think she's an awful musician," Laura added. "That's what I'm saying."

"No, but she *is* using her magic to help her get to a place some people reach without any magic at all." Emily shrugged. "Not a lot, but some. And nobody knows about that part."

"Honestly, I wouldn't even know how to try separating them to find out. But that's what Emily's saying, Laura. Like this hypothetical magician, we're all working with our magic in a way that makes us good at what we love to do, right? Or maybe we love it because of our magic. Either way, just like this magician who may or may not exist, we're witches, and we have jobs, and this is just one more way for us to blend in. 'Cause we have to."

"And in the end"—Emily spread her arms and grinned —"it doesn't even matter!" She laughed and attacked her chicken again.

Laura glanced between her sisters and frowned. "I get what you're saying. But using real magic to make everyone think you're amazing at using fake magic feels too much like cheating." A little shiver ran down her spine, and she shook her head. "Just talking about it makes me shiver."

Emily's fork clattered onto her plate when she threw her head back and laughed. "That really got to you, didn't it?"

Nickie chuckled, watching her older sister, and took another bite.

"All right, fine." Laura shook her head. "It got to me. Time to change the subject."

Nickie eyed her sideways for a moment, pretending to focus on her food rather than watching for Laura's reaction when she said, "We *could* talk about who called you earlier when Chuck was over."

Laura froze with her fork in her mouth. Both sisters watched her with wide eyes, waiting for her to chew, swallow, and come up with something to say. "What do you mean?"

"What does she *mean*?" Emily slapped a hand down on the table. "You're startin' to sound like Gilroy." She puffed out her chest and stuck out her bottom lip, frowning in her imitation of the snarky talking bust in their house who only answered what he deemed to be asked in the perfectly correct way. "*Rephrase the question, witch. I don't speak idiot.*"

"Hey, she never actually asked me a question." Laura gestured at Nickie, who had to cover her mouth to keep her last bite of chicken from falling out.

"You're deflecting, so I'll rephrase for her," Emily said. "*Who* called you earlier when Chuck was over?"

"I don't have to answer that."

"No, but you *want* to, don't you?" Nickie wiggled her eyebrows and stuck out her tongue. "Here, lemme help. I remember hearing the name Nathan in there somewhere."

"Ooh, *Nathan*." Emily shoved a forkful of vegetables into her mouth. "Who's Nathan?"

"You guys…"

"And why are you hiding him from us?" Nickie added.

"Oh, my god. Fine. He's the physics professor who moved into the empty office across the hall."

"Oh, nice." Emily bobbed her head and added in a teasing, singsong voice, "The physics professor called you on the phone." Her brow then furrowed. "Wait…the dwarf?"

"What?"

"Short, magical dudes with long beards who live underground?"

Nickie chuckled. "Well, not when they're teaching college-level physics."

"That doesn't make sense." Emily shook a finger at her oldest sister. "Were you lying about not being into short guys?"

"Okay. Stop." Laura dropped her fork, sat back, and raised her hands in surrender. "I wasn't gonna tell you guys because I knew you'd do *this*."

"Oh, come on. We've never done *this* before." Nickie reached out and gave Laura's shoulder a little pat.

"It took twenty-seven years, but our big sister is finally getting phone calls from boys." Emily blinked. "Men. Dwarf men."

Laura sighed and closed her eyes. "It's not that big of a deal, and there's nothing going on."

"So why did he call you?" Nickie shook her sister's shoulder this time. "Huh? What'd he have to say?"

After enough jostling, Laura finally cracked a smile. She jerked her shoulder out of Nickie's grasp just the same. "He called to ask me to a party..."

"Yes!" Emily pumped a fist. "And you told him yes, right?"

"No, I told him I'd think about it."

"And then you're gonna tell him yes."

"I don't *know*, Em, okay? I'm still thinking."

Nickie burst out laughing and pushed Laura's shoulder one more time. "You're blushing."

"Cut it out."

"When's the party?" Emily dropped her elbows on the table, rested her chin on her interlaced fingers, and batted her eyelashes.

"Tomorrow."

"A Sunday-night party, huh?" Nickie winked. "Good thing it's summer."

CHAPTER TWENTY

"I don't know about you guys," Laura said as she slid the last plate into the dishwasher and pushed it closed, "but I'm ready to pass out."

"You're actually going to bed, though, right?" Emily stuffed the new trash liner into the trashcan and dusted off her hands. "Like, you're not gonna go running around trying to destroy all these energy cores *by yourself* now that we know how to do it?"

Laura turned around with wide eyes. "I got way too little sleep last night with way too much alcohol in my body."

Nickie snorted.

"*And* I went who knows how far underground below a children's museum to dismantle an energy core before coming back here and spending about thirty seconds thinking you didn't make it out of that cavern. Plus, I had to help Nickie lie to Chuck about our weapons—"

"Hey…"

"And watch you slice up your hands fighting an antique suit of armor."

Emily shook her head. "It was hardly a fight."

"That doesn't make it better, Em." Laura laughed, because at this point, that was pretty much all she could do. "I'm tired. And we still have to destroy more energy cores. I'm thinking the airport next. For obvious reasons. So, no, I'm not going off by myself. I'm going to bed." She paused on her way through the dining room and turned slowly around. "Okay, so *if* I decide to go to that party tomorrow…would you guys wanna come with me?"

"Hmm…" Emily stroked her chin like she had a long beard to stroke and looked at the ceiling. "Totally. I should be off work at, like, four."

"Is this a plus-one kinda thing? Or should we just keep it to the three of us?" Nickie asked.

"I have no idea. But I guess I'll find out when I tell him I'm coming."

Emily elbowed Nickie in the ribs. "She's gonna tell him. She's saying yes to a date."

"It's not a date," Laura called from the stairs. "It's a party." She put one foot in front of the other and wondered why there were so many more stairs tonight than normal. "A party for a part-Kashgar physics professor who somehow mistook my repeated rejections yesterday for flirting," she muttered under her breath. "Unless I was flirting, and I have absolutely no idea what I'm doing. Yeah, I definitely need sleep."

. . .

Emily turned toward Nickie with a grin. "She's totally going on a date."

"Hey, you might be too."

"Huh?"

Nickie shrugged. "If this Nathan guy says, 'Yeah, sure. Go for it and bring lots of friends'…are you gonna bring John?"

"What, like a purse? Just sling him over my shoulder and bring him along with me?"

"I mean…if that's what works for you guys." Nickie huffed out a soundless laugh.

Emily snorted. "Maybe I'll *ask* if he wants to come. I dunno. You gonna *bring* Chuck?"

"Guess that depends on whether or not this is a magicals-only kinda party, right? Same goes for John too."

"Right." Blinking slowly, Emily turned toward her sister and frowned. "I never actually thought about that. You having to hide all this witchy-sister stuff from Chuck. That just feels like part of the whole thing you got goin' on."

"Trust me. It's not."

"Yeah, I think I realized that like two seconds ago. I wonder how many magicals fall in love with humans and spend the rest of their lives trying to hide it."

Nickie clenched her eyes shut and shook her head. "Not something I wanna even *start* thinking about right now."

"It does seem kinda…sad."

"Come on, Em."

"Okay, okay. I'm done." Emily headed toward the staircase and grabbed the banister. "I think I'm just gonna crash too. Work and stuff in the morning."

"Yeah, out of all of us, you got tossed around the most today."

"Ha. Not really. Just got caught up in an underground explosion and flayed my hands open with an iron-chain attached to a wrecking ball." Emily tossed her head back with an exaggerated laugh. "Happens all the time."

Nickie chuckled. "'Night, Em."

"'Night. Oh, hey." The youngest Hadstrom sister turned around on the staircase and leaned back a little. "What were you gonna say earlier about a big break with your music?"

"Oh." Nickie shook her head with a dismissive wave. "I'll tell you later. Go get some sleep."

"Okay. But don't forget." Emily almost ran up the staircase, pulling herself along by the banister.

Nickie sighed and rubbed the back of her neck. "Getting a record deal kinda feels like the least important thing going on right now. I'll just tell 'em when it actually happens." She stepped into the living room and grabbed her acoustic off the couch before spinning and flopping onto the cushions. She played a few chords, making it up as she went along, when she realized she recognized the song and couldn't remember how long she'd been playing their Dad's lullaby. She bolted upright and almost threw the guitar across the room. "Crap. No." Nickie shook her head. "What was I thinking?"

For a few minutes, she waited for the Gorafrex's primal drumbeat to burst into her head, seeing as she'd just played the song passed down through generations of Hadstrom witches and wizards and composed to *call* the creature. Yet, nothing happened, and Nickie relaxed a little. *Can't relax all the way, though. Obviously. If I had a better handle on how to play that magical lullaby without passing out, we'd probably have that thing locked up by now.*

She sighed and rubbed her face. "And I have no idea how to *get* a better handle on it." Then she froze, dropped her hands, and blinked. "But Dad might." Nickie whipped her phone out of the back pocket of her black skinny jeans and pulled up the text thread with her Dad.

'What are you doing tonight?'

He replied right away. *'Jam sesh.'* Greg Hadstrom followed that wannabe-cool text with an emoji of a guitar and a smiley face with sunglasses. *'You?'*

Nickie snorted. *'L and E went to bed. Super fun Saturday night at home.'*

'What about Chuck?'

'Dinner meeting, I think.'

The three little dots in the bottom corner of her screen blinked on, off, and on again until they stayed there for a really long time. With a sigh, Nickie dropped her phone on the couch. "I can't believe my dad has a better social life than I do." Then his next text came through.

'Wanna join us?'

Nickie did not expect him to send a picture of him, Ken, and Ronnie—the keyboardist and saxophonist who'd played with her the night before—sitting on a porch, drinks in hand as they toasted the camera. "Oh, man." Nickie laughed and typed in a reply.

'You look like a bunch of crazies. Gibson or Strat?'

'Both!'

"Seriously? Why not, I guess..."

'Send me the address.'

Her dad's reply came with an address, which she located on her nav app. "Of course. I bet Dad hasn't left the East Side in six months. Except for Emily's college graduation. And I'm about to walk right into it." Nickie stood and shoved her phone into her pocket, then grabbed her Gibson acoustic from behind the couch and stuck it in its case. Next came her dark-blue Deluxe Strat off the guitar stand and into its case. She locked them both and stood with a handle in each hand. "Too early for bed, anyway."

Nickie stopped at the front door and sighed since she didn't have enough hands to hold them *and* turn the handle. Right on cue, the black ring flashed on her thumb, and the door slowly opened. "Okay, I'm really startin' to dig you, ring." With a nod, she stepped outside into Austin's balmy night air, and her legacy ring pulled the door softly shut behind her.

In her bedroom, Emily fiddled with the thumbprint coin on her keyring, weighing the pros against the cons. "Kind of a no-brainer, really." She glanced at Speed sleeping on the bed beside her. "Did you get up *at all* since you jumped into our first transport bubble?" Of course, the immortally lazy bulldog gave no reply. Rolling her eyes, she stared at her keyring. "So, if I did this, Laura would be totally surprised. In a good way, I think. And there's no way Laura Hadstrom, lover of all magical artifacts, would give up the opportunity to add another to her collection. That thing was seriously powerful."

Speed snorted in his sleep and puffed out a doggy sigh.

"You're right. I should just do it, get it over with, and

she'll thank me more than lecture me, right? Okay." Emily stood and stuck her keys into her back pocket. "Just in case. Probably won't even need it."

She closed her eyes and focused on the giant energy core beneath the Thinkery. "At least I know exactly where I'm going this time." She shot Speed a devious grin, and before she could even mutter the spell, a shimmering transport bubble bloomed from her flashing copper ring and grew in the middle of her bedroom.

CHAPTER TWENTY-ONE

Nickie pulled up to the two-story house on the East Side just before 11:00 p.m. The lights were on, cars parked all up and down the street, and the steady thump of drums and bass with the occasional squeal of an electric guitar washed over all of it. She thumped her head back against the headrest and turned off the engine. "Here we go."

When she opened her trunk, she decided to just go with the Gibson for now. *Don't wanna overdo it. And I don't even really know what they're getting up to in there.* Her guitar case felt light in her hand as she stepped up onto the sidewalk . Knocking on the front door—twice—didn't bring anyone to answer it, but at least it was unlocked. Nickie pushed the door open and stepped into what was the weirdest and most nostalgically familiar party she could remember.

"Oh, my God." She glanced around and couldn't help but laugh. The house was immaculate, well-decorated, pictures on the mantle in the living room too far away for her to see anyone's faces. There weren't any strobing lights or flashy effects like the few frat parties she'd gone to right out of high school before deciding they were not her thing.

What surprised her most, people milled about everywhere. Both couches in the living room were packed with four people each, everyone with a clear plastic cup in hand as they passed around what had to be a joint. They talked and laughed, having a great time without the rowdiness of parties with younger guests.

Nickie grinned as she stepped into the house. She lifted a hand when everyone in the living room waved and said hi. "I'm totally the youngest person here," she muttered. "Feels like I'm ten again, except now I'm actually invited—" She almost bumped into a woman in a flowing shirt and gray pants exiting the bathroom. "Whoops. Sorry."

"All good, honey. All good." The woman grinned, patted Nickie on the shoulder, and moved on.

The kitchen was packed, and Nickie didn't recognize a single face until she saw Ronnie's wife at the kitchen island scooping a massive pile of seven-layer dip onto a clear plastic plate. "Hey, Margot."

The woman looked up and squealed. "Nickie! Girl, I am so *glad* you actually came! Come here." She dropped the plate on the island and slipped through the other women standing with her, who all smiled as Margot wrapped Nickie in a tight hug. Nickie found it a little awkward trying to hug her back with her guitar case in hand.

Margot pulled away and grabbed her shoulders. "I saw the show last night."

"Oh, yeah?" Nickie laughed. "How was it?"

"Between you and me? The band hasn't changed a bit in

fifteen years." They both laughed. "But *you?* Mm! Girl, you're even better than your daddy."

Nickie grinned. "I'll take it."

"You better. And he knows it. He would not stop *talking* about you coming over. I had to bring my ass in off the back porch just so I could hear myself think again."

"This is your place?"

"Mm-hmm. Been here for twenty-five years. You didn't know that?"

Nickie shook her head. "I haven't been around as long as…most people here."

Margot threw let out a sharp laugh. "Now you're just making me feel old. Come on. Let's go. They're all outside waitin' for you to show 'em how it's done." The woman nodded at the sliding glass door off the back of the kitchen. With a smile and a few nods and hellos to the other party-goers, Nickie followed Margot to the back porch.

Tiki torches emanated light from around the perimeter of the back yard, plus some strings of lights decorated the top of the screened-in porch and wrapped around the framing posts. Two rocking chairs, a glider, two wicker armchairs, and an outdoor dining set took up half the space, and every seat but one armchair had someone sitting in it. The men burst out laughing at someone's joke.

"Look at you." Margot tossed her hands in the air. "Crackin' up out here, and not one of you thought to tell this woman whose house she was comin' to?"

The laughter died down as Ronnie, Ken, Nickie's dad, and a lanky man in a cowboy hat turned their attention to the woman standing there with her hands on her hips. "Nickie!" Greg stood and flung his arms open to hug his daughter, nearly smacking Ken in the face. The keyboardist waved Greg's hand away, chuckling, and Nickie stepped into the hug.

"Hey, Dad."

"You didn't know this was Ronnie and Margot's place?"

"Nope."

"Bet you wouldn't have guessed it, huh?" Ronnie grinned from one of the rocking chairs. "I'd be happy living in a shack, but Margot kept going on and on about high expectations. Whatever those are."

Margot clicked her tongue. "Please. You were living in a shack when I met you." The men burst out laughing, shaking their heads. "Don't act like you don't appreciate those high expectations, either. Since you're the one showin' 'em off tonight."

Ken let out a low whistle and raised his clear plastic cup to his lips, chuckling.

Their hostess cocked her head at Nickie and raised an eyebrow. One long, burgundy-painted fingernail pointed at the men on the porch. "When you get tired of all these hotshots spoutin' off about their glory days instead of livin' in 'em, come find me."

"Yeah, okay." Nickie grinned.

Margot shot her a wink before raising an eyebrow at her husband and his friends. "Y'all got the real deal standin' in front of you now. Don't forget."

"Boy, don't we know it," Ken said in his deep, drawling voice before taking another sip of his drink. Margot slipped back inside through the sliding glass doors, and Greg gave his daughter's shoulder a squeeze.

"Come sit down, Nickie."

"Yeah, take a load off."

She laughed and took the empty armchair as her dad returned to the rocking chair. The guitar case settled on the porch beside her, and she leaned back, lifting both arms onto the armrests. "So this is your jam session, huh?"

They laughed and shifted around in their seats. "Well, that's what it started out as." Ronnie nodded at his saxophone case lying on the table runner on the patio table.

"Man, you can't say it started as anything if we didn't actually play."

"At least I got my instrument farther than the front door."

Nickie chuckled. "But you live here."

Ronnie wheezed out a laugh and lifted his plastic cup toward her. "Touché. Hey, you drinkin' anything?"

"Not yet."

"Greg. Grab that bottle of bourbon and get your kid a drink."

Another round of chuckling filled the porch as Nickie's dad leaned over the side of the rocking chair and picked up a bottle of bourbon. "You good with this?"

Nickie smirked. "Oh, yeah."

"Of *course* she's good with it," Ronnie said. "Nickie can handle anything."

"Including showin' up blues legend Greg Hadstrom, the way I hear it." The man in the cowboy hat rocked on the glider and crossed one pointy-toed boot over his bony knee.

"Nickie, did I ever introduce you to Bobby Rawlin?" Greg lifted the beer bottle toward his friend.

"You just did." Nickie nodded at the man in the cowboy hat. "Nice to meet you, Bobby."

"You too, darlin'."

"Maybe now your old man'll quit tellin' us everything we know about you." Ronnie chuckled. "Guess that's what we get for playin' with two different legends in two different decades, huh?"

"Oh, man." Nickie grinned. "I'm not a legend."

"But you will be, kid."

Greg glanced around at the patio floor and then at the table beside him. "Anybody got an extra cup around here?"

"Ronnie, what's in here?" Ken pointed to the mostly full cup on the low wicker side table between them.

"Water."

Ken reached out with a grunt, grabbed the cup, and tossed the water through the screen into the yard.

"*My* water, man."

"Naw, you got a bourbon in your hand, Ronnie. You don't need water."

"Tell that to the heartburn."

"Yeah, just keep drinking. That'll clear it right up." With a smirk, Ken leaned forward and passed the plastic cup to Nickie's dad, who was just sober enough to pour two fingers of bourbon into it without spilling any.

"Here you go, my musical genius of a daughter."

Nickie took the cup and lifted it toward her dad. "If I drink this, will your compliments get any better?"

Ronnie howled with laughter, slapping his knee. Ken smirked into his bourbon again, and Bobby kept rocking on the glider, his head bent low so only his smirk was visible beneath the wide brim of his hat.

"You tell me, sweetheart." Greg set the bottle of bourbon on the ground and lifted his cup toward her. "I'm glad you came out."

"Mm-hmm." Ken lifted his cup, followed by Ronnie and Bobby, and a grinning Nickie joined the toast.

"To the new Queen of Blues," Ronnie added. "Nickie, I hope you own that stage as long as we have."

Ken leaned away from him and shot the man a sideways glance. "Man, you don't wanna go puttin' that on anybody." They all laughed again, ending the toast, and drank.

The bourbon burned down Nickie's throat, and she tilted her head. "I wouldn't be where I am without the three of you."

"Sorry, Bobby." Ken grinned at the man on the glider. "You just haven't proven yourself worthy, yet."

Bobby kept rocking and shook his head. "Only 'cause I ain't overcompensatin' like the rest of you." The other men groaned and waved him off, and the smirk returned beneath the cowboy hat.

"That's a kind thing to say, Nickie," Ronnie said. "But we all know you'd be movin' on up with or without us."

Nickie shrugged. "I learned everything I know from watching you guys. And playing with you guys. I thought you'd *wanna* take a little bit of the glory."

Ronnie grinned and winked at her. "Puttin' that charm on pretty thick, aren't ya?"

"Just for you, man." Nickie took another stinging sip of straight bourbon.

"How 'bout the real charm, though?" Ken set his drink down on the side table, braced his hands against his thighs, and pushed himself up out of the chair. "Before anyone says anything, I'll go get my damn keyboard." The other men chuckled.

"How 'bout it, Nickie?" Her dad gazed at her with his head tilted, his eyes shining more than usual, accentuated by how much he'd had to drink.

"Not a real jam session without me, huh?"

Ronnie hooted and stood to grab his sax from the table, shaking his head. "Guess not."

They both pulled their instruments from their cases, and Nickie slipped her favorite lime-green pick out from between the Gibson's strings on the fretboard. By the time she'd finished a casual tuning, Ken came huffing back with his full-sized keyboard in tow and the cables slung over his shoulder. He *thunked* it down onto the table and plugged his set into the outlet on the porch.

Margot stuck her head out of the patio door he hadn't closed and raised an eyebrow at them. "And y'all just thought he wouldn't need any help with that thing?"

"He never does, baby."

"Probably 'cause he'd never ask." Margot shook her head. "Just shut the door behind you, huh? Bunch of grown men acting like animals around here." Chuckling, she slipped back inside, closing the sliding door behind her.

"All right. I'm good." Ken waved a hand at them and turned on the keyboard.

"Just take it, Nickie," Ronnie said, nodding.

She struck up something in D minor. After a few beats, Ken joined in with the keyboard. Ronnie's head swiveled as he bobbed in the chair, and the minute he started playing, Bobby reached into the front pocket of his plaid button-down shirt. Nickie caught a brief flash of something in the light before the main wailed away on a harmonica.

She laughed. "That's so awesome."

Greg sat back in the rocking chair and closed his eyes.

"You wanna go after this?" she asked him, her energy somewhere between wanting to stand and being perfectly happy sitting.

"You play as long as you want, kiddo. I'm good." He lifted his bourbon for another drink.

Nickie smiled and played, but the smile faded a little when she remembered why she'd come out in the first place. *I just hope he's not too drunk to help me out after this.*

CHAPTER TWENTY-TWO

Emily's transport bubble popped, and she found herself in complete darkness. "Good thing I've been here before." Before the spell even reached her lips, a muted copper light flashed on her ring, and a glowing orb appeared in her palm. "These rings are so *cool.*" She lifted the light, where it grew enough for her to see the giant expanse of the chamber they'd barely escaped earlier that afternoon.

"Holy cow…" She looked around. The energy core she'd destroyed with her sisters lay a few yards in front of her at an angle. The glass-like material of the huge column had fractured in the middle, most likely when it toppled against the far wall of the chamber. Clear, shattered fragments were strewn all over, reflecting her orb of light from thousands of glittering pieces. And Laura's teal bowling ball remained wedged into the top half of the energy core. The metal base of the column had partly ripped from its moorings, and everything was silent.

"Okay. So where is it?" Emily turned in a slow circle,

knowing she didn't have to look on the other side of the fallen structure. With a gentle wave of her hand, her floating light descended and came closer. There, on the floor under where the core had crashed against the wall, lay the two-foot iron socket wrench the Velikan Engineer gave Laura.

"Found you…" Emily grinned. "Not lettin' you get away. We need whatever kinda magic you have. We need something that packs a punch—"

A shadow flickered in the corner of her vision, though her light hovered still above her. A loud, angry hiss filled the chamber. *"No!"* That one growling, enraged word became many as it echoed between the walls of stone and iron. "What *is* this?" The shadow moved, growing shorter as a woman with matted brown hair and a ripped and stained dress stepped through the arch made by the fallen energy core.

Emily froze. *That is definitely not a witch…*

The woman sniffed the air, then jerked her head toward Emily and locked gazes with her. *"You,"* the woman spat, her eyes flashing bright silver.

"Crap." The minute Emily glanced down at the Velikan socket wrench just a few yards away, the Gorafrex's ancient, frenzied drumbeat burst through the chamber, yet only for a few seconds.

Why'd it stop? Emily's breath hitched in her throat. She eyed the Gorafrex inside its current host. The woman's face contorted in rage and confusion as she stepped toward the Gorafrex's intended victim.

"Uh-uh." Emily stretched her hand out toward the socket wrench. With a flash from her ring, the heavy iron rod shot through the air and into her hands. She caught it, but the force knocked the Velikan tool into her chest with a *thud*. "Ow."

The Gorafrex hissed through human teeth. The woman picked up the pace toward Emily, and the drumbeat resumed.

The young witch whirled away from the chamber and the broken energy core. She took off down the passageway. *This thing is too freakin' heavy.* Her breathing echoed around her, while the orb of light darted on her heels.

The drums stopped. And an unnerving silence followed. Emily couldn't help glancing over her shoulder. The Gorafrex stood in the entryway to the chamber, its human host's arms outstretched. For a second, the woman's body shimmered with opalescent light, which spread around her in an aura.

"I'm not *finished*," the woman roared. The shimmering light around her shrank into her body, and the drumming renewed with full force. "You're mine."

Emily hefted the socket wrench into the crook of her arm and snatched her keyring from her back pocket. "Nope." She glared at the Gorafrex storming toward her, even while the frantic, primal drumbeat shook the passage walls. Her thumb slipped into place on the silver coin, and she disappeared.

The socket wrench toppled out of her arm as she stumbled backward inside the Clubhouse. "Oh, my *god*. What the—crap. Crap. Crap!" Emily spun in a tight circle and grasped her head with both hands, trying to still her heavy breathing. "Definitely the Gorafrex. Inside another host."

She dragged her hands down her cheeks and groaned.

"As far as I know, that's three humans it's worn around town." Fighting back a shiver of disgust, she stooped to pick up the huge socket wrench and took it with her to the cherry-red futon. "That was close. That was *way* too close. Come on, Emily. Why don't you *think* first? That thing had no idea we already destroyed the energy core. Of *course* it would show up eventually to get things ready for the next…" She groaned. "The next witch. It's gonna go after one soon. Like, really soon."

She slumped against the futon and closed her eyes. "I made it out. Okay, Clubhouse, I'm officially more grateful for you now than any other point in my life."

Sliding the socket wrench off her lap until it landed on the cushion, Emily opened her eyes and sat up. "We found the murdered witch and the last human host on…Tuesday. Five days ago. But now it's…what? Being pushed out of that woman's body?" She chewed on her lower lip and frowned. "Same thing happened when we found it in that man with the ponytail. The shimmering thing right before it left him and went into the woman in the parking lot. So, it's keeping its hosts longer and longer each time, but it still can't stay…"

She gave the socket wrench a dubious glance. "If it's trying to stay inside that woman, we might have more time. Unless it slithers into someone else. I have to tell Laura and Nickie."

Emily pushed up off the couch and paced across the room. She fingered the coin on her keyring. "We need to —" The keys jingled in her hand when she shook them. "I need to calm down. Wait a little bit. That thing could still be there, but it won't stay all night if it's too weak to keep its host much longer. Okay…" With a deep breath, she sighed and nodded. "I can hang out for a while. Then I'll pull up another transport bubble home. Easy."

Emily paced across the Clubhouse floor another ten minutes. It felt more like ten days.

"This isn't easy at all. What am I *doing*?" She lifted her keyring and glanced at the copper ring on her thumb. "I know I can time it perfectly."

She slipped her thumb over the coin and left the one place that kept witches safe from the ancient, powerful creature.

CHAPTER TWENTY-THREE

After an hour of a few long songs, a bit of singing, and some incredible solos by all four of them, the humidity had got to her. Nickie's dark-red tank top clung to her skin as much as the hair around her face and at the back of her neck. Thanks to the bourbon—and she'd only drunk half of what her dad poured her—all of that was easy to ignore. For a while.

Ronnie lowered his saxophone by the strap around his head, blew out a long breath, and shook his head. "Used to be I could stay up 'til sunrise doin' this."

"Really?" Ken stepped sideways down the table to lean over it on his hands beside the keyboard. "You were sittin' the whole damn time, man."

"And maybe it's the sittin' that got to me." Ronnie chuckled and pushed himself up out of the chair. "Knees aren't what they used to be. Greg, you and I used to jump around stage like a couple of skinny punks. Remember?"

Nickie's dad waved a dismissive hand and grunted, his eyes still closed. "I remember everything."

"Yeah, I bet you do." Ken chuckled. "Especially now. And I just remembered I need to eat."

"*Oh*, yeah." Ronnie turned to put his saxophone back in the case, then brought it over to the table. "Margot put out a huge tray of barbeque. I hear it callin' my name."

Ken clicked his tongue. "Man, and you didn't think to tell us about barbeque before we came out here?"

"You walked right through the kitchen. I ain't your momma, Kennie boy. You can feed your own damn self." Laughing, they both turned toward the sliding glass door. "Anyone else need to fill their belly?"

"Yup." Bobby's harmonica slipped into the front pocket of his shirt, and he stood from the glider in one fluid movement.

Nickie looked at him with a grin. *That is the tallest person I've ever seen.* When he passed her, she saw the glint of Bobby's eyes beneath the shadow of his cowboy hat. He tipped the brim at her and winked without stopping his slow, lanky stride.

"Nickie? Greg? Y'all want somethin'?"

"No, thanks." Nickie turned in the armchair and nodded at them. "I ate right before I came over. Dad?"

"I'm good, babycakes," he said to her.

Ronnie slid open the door. "I'm tellin' ya, Margot's brisket can make a man do unspeakable things. You don't know what you're missin'."

"And we don't know if *we* missed it," Ken added as they stepped inside. "Invite a man over to your house and not tell him your wife made—" The door slid shut behind them.

Nickie chuckled. "They're like an old married couple, those two."

Her dad snorted and tossed his hand. "They were at each other like that twenty years ago. Just keeps getting' worse the older they get." His eyes opened slowly, and he blinked. "If that's what bein' an old married couple is like, I'm *glad* I won't be spending the last of my days bickering with anyone."

Because he and Mom spent the last days of their marriage doing it instead. I can't believe he's bringing that up right now. "Dad…"

"Sorry, kiddo." Greg turned his head to fix her with shining eyes just a little red-rimmed from all the bourbon in his veins. "I shouldn't be sayin' stuff like that in front of you."

"Thank you." Nickie sat back in her chair again, picked at a few chords on her Gibson, and stopped. "Dad, I have a question for you."

"Shoot."

Okay, here we go. Let's hope he's not too drunk to give me a coherent answer. "When you were wearing this ring…" They both glanced at the black legacy ring on her thumb, which he'd worn most his life until almost two weeks ago, when the Hadstrom family legacy and the responsibilities that came with it were passed to his three daughters. "Did it do anything weird with your music?"

Greg laughed and sailed back and forth in the rocking chair. "I told you girls these rings would make your magic stronger, didn't I?"

"Yeah, you did."

"Good. Yeah, Nickie, I had a few strange experiences

with it when I was first figuring out how to be a wizard and a Hadstrom *and* an up-and-coming musician all at the same time."

"Really?"

"Mm-hmm." His eyes drooped closed as he rocked, and he cleared his throat. "I remember playin' a show one night. I must've been…oh, twenty-four. Twenty-five, maybe. Right after I met your mom and we were still figuring each other out."

Please don't give any details on that. *Not now.*

Greg chuckled. "I had the worst head cold of my life at that point. All stuffed up. Head swimmin'. Could barely open my eyes, I was so dizzy."

"And you still did the show."

"Of course I still did the show. That's what we do, kiddo. The show must go on…" He laughed and shook his head. "I *really* hate that sayin'."

"Gotta love clichés, though, right?" Nickie grinned.

"No you don't." Greg smirked. "But it fits. Now…weird things with the ring and my music? Oh, yeah. I was sicker'n a dog that night. Thought I'd fall over the minute we walked on. Even *before* the lights felt like they were burnin' me to Kingdom Come. Then I started playin', 'cause that's what we do." He paused, still rocking back and forth.

"Dad?"

He took a sharp breath. "Yeah."

"Keep going."

"Oh. Right, right. Yeah…" He paused a few seconds, then exhaled. "I didn't think I could do it, Nickie. But then, when I played, I felt it."

"Felt what?"

"The *magic*. Oh, it was always there, sure. Can't help that I'm a wizard. Can't help it you're a witch. That magic's in our blood. But that ring grew warm on my finger, and once I started playin', I couldn't stop."

That sounds like what happened to me at Tina's laundromat. "You think the ring was doing that?"

"I *know* the ring was doing that. Those things…well, like I said, they make our magic stronger. Channel it. Bend it to a more specific purpose. That's what they were made for in the very, very beginning. Damn, it's crazy to think how long ago that was." Greg sucked in a short breath, tucked his chin, and let out a soft burp. Then he laughed and put a fist to his chest. "'Scuse me. Anyway, when that ring tapped into my magic and…magnified it, it completely took over, you understand? I played the hell outta that show, and the whole time, I kept thinking about how much I wanted to stop and lie down for just a few minutes. Didn't matter. The magic wouldn't let me. I thought I was gonna drop dead backstage at the end of it. Then Ronnie…" Greg laughed and shook his head. "Ronnie told me that was the best he'd ever seen me play. Said I was on *fire*. I realized I had to figure out a way to stop the damn thing from overwhelming me like that again. Had to figure out how to control it, yeah?"

"That's exactly what I'm trying to do." Nickie nodded. *If I end up playing that lullaby to call the Gorafrex again, I can't let what happened last time happen. I was useless.*

"It already took you over, huh?" Her dad stopped rocking long enough to meet her gaze.

"Yeah. Just once." Nickie shrugged. "I think I passed out and slept for…I'm not sure, actually. Felt like days."

"Yep. That's it."

"So how did you learn to control it?"

Greg chuckled. "Trial and error, kiddo."

Great. I don't have time for trial and error.

"That's it?"

"No. I can pass my learnin' on to you, can't I? Good thing you and I share the same kinda magic. Your grandpa was the furthest thing from a musician. Architect for the city. All that building and planning. I could never wrap my brain around half the math that man did in his head just like that." Greg snapped his fingers. "If I'd been able to go to my daddy when I was figuring out this ring stuff… whew. Would've saved me a lotta trouble."

"Not as much as it'll save me."

"Don't be so hard on yourself, Nickie. You'll get there."

"Dad."

"Yeah, babe?"

Nickie forced herself not to get aggravated with him. "How'd you learn to control it?"

"I realized what my music really was." He cleared his throat and kept rocking in the chair. "The whole time, I thought being a wizard just made me a better musician. That my magic *fed* my music, yeah? But it's the other way around, Nickie. Music *is* a form of magic, you understand? Music *fuels* the other parts of us. We wouldn't be who we are without it. Sure, there are even some humans who've gotten as close to wielding that kinda magic in its purest form. But we…*we* get to use it the way we want. When you think about it like that, kiddo, the whole game changes. Instead of the music moving *you*, you move the magic. Play your music like you're casting a spell, not like you're escaping something. Do that, and you'll be unstoppable."

"Oh…" *For as drunk as he is, that makes perfect sense.*

"Does that make sense?"

"Absolutely. That's exactly what I needed to hear. Thanks, Dad."

"Anything for you, kiddo. I'm glad you asked." Greg dropped his arm over the side of the armrest and patted her knee. "You're all the best parts of me wrapped up into one, you know that? You've never had my shortcomings, Nickie. That's what's gonna take you anywhere you wanna go in this world." He squeezed her knee, and she covered it with her hand.

"Well, thanks." When he opened his eyes to look at her, she smiled. Her dad's lips curled up into a crooked grin. "I'm definitely not perfect, though."

"You are to me."

"Yeah, I bet you say that to all your daughters." They both laughed. "I think Laura's the only one who—" A sharp pain burst behind her eyes, and she swallowed. "Who—" Three seconds of that ancient, primal drumbeat pounded in her head, like the opening echo of a gladiator match or some old, dark ceremony about to begin. Nickie clenched her eyes shut and tried to fight through the pain.

"You okay?"

She sighed, but it came out more like a grunt. "Yeah. I've just been getting these really bad migraines late—" The drums pounded louder and faster and suddenly stopped, yet the pressure kept building behind and between her eyes.

"I'm sorry, kiddo. I bet Margot's got some aspirin or

somethin'. Want me to go check?" Greg shifted in the rocking chair like he was about to get up.

Nickie patted his arm. "No, Dad. I'm okay."

"You should still take something."

She shook her head. "I've got something in the car. And I should probably get going anyway. It's…what? Almost one o'clock."

"Is it really? Hoo, boy." Greg snorted and shook his head. "Feels like the sun should be comin' up."

"Yeah, I'm gonna go." Nickie stood, blinking furiously against the lights strung across the porch.

"If it's that bad, Nickie, you should stay here. I know Ronnie and Margot have an extra room. Or at least rest until that headache goes. I don't like the thought of you drivin' like this."

"I'll be fine. Promise. It's just a little one. If I take something now, I'll be okay." She set her guitar into its case, locked it, and stepped toward his chair. "Thanks for inviting me. I needed this."

"We did too. Old-folk parties aren't nearly as fun as they used to be when we were younger." He laughed. "Well, they were young-folk parties, then. Seein' you play reminds me of how many good things this world still has to offer, you know that?"

Nickie forced herself to smile through the migraine. "I do now." She bent and placed a kiss on his warm, scruffy cheek. He smelled like bourbon fumes and soap. "Love you, Dad."

"I love you too, Nickie." He patted her arm, then leaned back in the rocking chair again. "You be safe."

"I will." She picked up her case and headed for the

sliding door. *I really hope this goes away like last night. Probably shoulda told my sisters the truth.*

There were fewer people inside the house now. Music still played through their surround sound in the living room. Ronnie, Ken, Bobby, Margot, and two other people she didn't know stood around the kitchen island, digging into what was left of Margot's barbeque.

"You change your mind about the brisket?" Ronnie asked with a grin.

"I'm sure it's amazing." Nickie shook her head. "No, I'm headin' out."

Ken choked on his bite and leaned over the clear plastic plate in his hand. "Well now I've seen everything. A musician in her prime turnin' in before us ancients." He wheezed out a laugh.

Margot slapped his arm with the back of her hand. "Speak for yourself." She turned to Nickie. "Drive safe. You feelin' okay?"

"What? Yeah." Nickie gave the woman a hug. "Thanks for having me over, Margot."

"Anytime, girl." The woman pulled back and studied Nickie's face with concern. "You sure you're okay? Your color doesn't look so good."

"Just tired. I was up late last night too." Nickie nodded at everyone smiling at her. "Bobby, nice to meet you."

"Pleasure, darlin'."

"And I'll see you two in a few days, right? Next show?"

Ronnie nodded, and Ken swallowed his mouthful. "As long as Chuck hasn't decided to replace us." He winked. "We'll be there."

"Good. Thanks again."

"'Night, Nickie."

Their conversation started up again as she headed through the house toward the front door. A few feet before she reached it, the drumming blasted into her head, fast and urgent, desperate. Calling. It lasted twice as long this time. Nickie staggered sideways and almost dropped the guitar case.

"Woah." Three people on the couches in the living room definitely saw her. "Hey, you okay?"

"Yeah." Nickie caught her breath and tried to smile. "Just tired."

"Didn't have too much to drink, did you?"

"Definitely not." She turned, smiling through the pounding throb growing behind her eyes, and touched her nose with her finger. She took a few steps toward the living room in a perfectly straight line and nodded. "I'm not drunk. Just tired."

"Okay…" The man grinning at her glanced at her steady feet and nodded. "Be safe."

"Thanks. Y'all have a good night." Nickie couldn't get out of there fast enough.

The minute she pulled the front door shut, she booked it down the walkway and to her car. Fewer cars were on the residential street, and most houses were dark. She brought her guitar case with her when she slipped behind the wheel and placed it gently in the passenger seat. Then she shut the door, stuck her keys in the ignition, and sighed. "Good thing this started *after* Dad gave me a few tips." She strapped on her seatbelt and drove slowly down the street. "Other than that, this is the worst timing ever."

The traffic lights on her drive west into downtown

didn't help the migraine, but she pushed through. Halfway home, though, the drums returned, each beat rattling her brain the way she could feel Marcus' bass drum and Melvin's low bassline rattling in her chest during a show.

Nickie's vision darkened. "Oh, god. I'm gonna hit something."

She pulled into a gas station lot. As soon as she turned the engine off, she jerked the keys out of the ignition, fighting to catch her breath, and pressed her thumb into the coin on her keyring.

Her skin tingled everywhere, and then she was sitting on the floor in the middle of the Clubhouse. The Gorafrex's luring and agonizing drumbeat cut off immediately. The headache remained, but at least she could hear herself think.

With a sigh of relief, Nickie stayed where she was in the middle of the room and lay back onto the floor. "Just for a little bit. Just until the headache's gone." She slowed her breathing and closed her eyes. "Then I'll tell Laura and Emily that thing's gonna start hunting again soon."

An hour later, she jolted awake. It took her a few seconds to remember where she was and why. "Oh, man. I still hafta drive home." Her keys were clutched in her hand. "Here's to no more drums." She pressed her thumb into the coin again, not once noticing the massive iron socket wrench lying on the cherry-red futon beside her. Then she disappeared.

Fortunately, neither the drums nor the migraine returned during the next ten minutes of her drive home.

Nickie grabbed her guitar case out of the passenger seat and headed up the concrete stairs set into the hillside toward the house. She sidled inside without hearing anything from her sisters, and wherever Speed was sleeping, he stayed where he was.

Leaving her guitar just inside the living room, she climbed the stairs with heavy eyelids, relieved to be back home and headed to her room. *At least my sisters are both here if something happens again.*

Nickie stripped off her clothes, crawled into bed, and dozed off with the keyring—her only means of escape from the Gorafrex—clutched in her hand.

CHAPTER TWENTY-FOUR

Laura jolted from her bed Sunday morning with a feeling of dread. "That's the first time I've *dreamt* about the drums..." A glance at her phone on the night-stand told her it was 6:03 a.m. "Okay, I got plenty of sleep. So why do I feel like something awful's about to happen?" She rolled out of bed, stuck her bare feet into her plain brown slippers, and headed out of her room in her pajamas.

The first thing she noticed when she walked down the hall was Emily's door wide open. "She never leaves it open..."

Stepping quietly toward her younger sister's room, Laura blinked the sleep out of her eyes and peered inside. "Em? You awake?" Something rustled on the foot of the bed, and Speed poked his head out of the wadded-up comforter. He grunted at her and disappeared again. "And now I see why she doesn't leave the door open."

Emily's room was a disaster, clothes flung everywhere, scattered papers across her desk, and the bed, of course, wasn't even a little made. Laura grabbed the door handle and pulled it shut, then turned toward the stairs.

Nickie's bedroom door opened, and her sister shuffled out in loose plaid pajama pants and an oversized t-shirt, her hair a tangled mess, and dark circles under her eyes.

"Woah, Nickie." Laura blinked. "What happened to you?"

"Huh?" Her sister slowly looked up at her. "Oh. I went out last night."

"After we went to bed?"

"Yep."

"Where did Chuck take you this time?"

Nickie smacked her lips, eyelids drooping and moved toward the staircase. "Chuck was at a dinner meeting, I think. I dunno how late. I went to the East Side instead."

"Who's on the East Side?"

"Dad. Ronnie and his wife were having a house party."

Laura snorted. "It was a bunch of people older than our parents, wasn't it?"

Her sister nodded. "It was weird but also cool. We played a little bit, and then I..." Finally, Nickie's eyes opened wide. She turned at the top of the stairs to stare at Laura. "I need to tell you something."

"Good or bad something?"

"Uh...both."

"Okay." Laura nodded toward the stairs, and they made their way down. "Emily didn't go with you, did she?"

"No. She went to bed when you did."

"Well, she's not in her room—"

"Hey! You're both awake!" Emily came skidding around

the dining room corner and into the foyer, grinning at them. "Excellent."

"You are *way* too chipper," Laura muttered.

"Weird, right? Only got a few hours sleep."

They made it down the staircase, warily eyeing their youngest sister as she bounced on the balls of her feet with way too much energy.

Nickie frowned. "When did you wake up?"

"I dunno. Four, maybe?" Emily shook her head and took off into the kitchen. "I couldn't sleep. But we really need to talk, guys. I...well, I need to tell you something you definitely wanna hear."

"Can it wait 'til after coffee?"

"Uh...are you *telling* me to wait?"

Laura raised an eyebrow at her sister and headed across the kitchen. "Do I need to?"

"No. Nope. Definitely not. I can wait. Oh, yeah. Just made another pot." She gestured toward the coffeemaker on the counter.

"*Another* pot?" Nickie squinted at her.

"That's what I said. I already had a few cups, so go crazy." Emily snickered and rubbed her hands together. "You look like you could use a few cups, Nick."

"Yeah, and you like you shouldn't touch coffee again for a week."

"Hey, that punishment in *no* way fits the crime."

Laura filled a mug and set it on the counter. "Why would you need a punishment?"

"What? I don't. I mean, I wouldn't." Emily sighed and pointed at the coffeemaker. "Just make your coffee already, okay?"

Nickie joined Laura at the counter and picked up the first cup. "She seem weird to you?" she muttered.

"Yeah, that's not *happy* Emily. That's slap-happy, hyped-up-on-caffeine Emily. What happened?"

"Guess we're about to find out." Nickie shrugged, then turned slowly toward the table as Laura grabbed the milk from the fridge to add to her sugar and coffee.

"Oh, my god. You guys move like frozen slugs." Emily stopped behind a chair at the kitchen table and drummed her fingers on the back of it. "Come on, Laura. I think you've stirred it enough."

"And *I* think I'm just gonna take my time, nice and slow this morning." Laura grinned at her youngest sister and lifted the mug to her lips with agonizing slowness. "Just to—"

"Just to mess with me. Yeah. I get it. Can you just..." Emily twirled her hand and bobbed her head in impatience.

"Hey, maybe you should sit down." Nickie nodded at the chair in front of her.

"What? Yeah. Good idea." Emily jerked the chair back and plopped into it, then drummed her fingers on the table.

"Em..."

"Sorry." She dropped her hands into her lap, then her knee started bouncing while she waited for Laura to join them.

"Okay." Laura slid into the other chair and took another sip. "So you both have something to say this morning, right?"

"We do?" Emily glanced at Nickie.

"Yeah, you go ahead." Nickie snorted. "I can wait. Doesn't look like you can."

"Cool. Thanks." Emily lifted her hands a little, dropped them in her lap, then decided to pull them up and fold them on the table. "I went back to the energy core under the Thinkery last night."

Laura choked on her coffee. "*What?*"

"Are you kidding me?" Nickie added.

"Not even a little." Emily cocked her head, her knee bouncing beneath the table. Then she took a deep breath. "Okay, to be fair, I knew it was a bad idea before I went."

"Then why did you—"

"I wanted to get that wrench thing. You know, the one the Engineer gave you."

Laura sighed. "Em, it's just a tool. That thing isn't worth risking yourself. Especially going back there alone."

"But did you see what it did?" Emily glanced back and forth between them with wide eyes. "One little tap, Laura, and that wrench brought the entire energy core crashing down."

"Yeah, and it almost took you with it."

"That's..." Emily sighed. "That's not the point. That *tool* is seriously powerful. We need it. It's the only thing that's pretty much guaranteed to break down the energy cores at this point, which we really need to start doing faster."

Laura shared a concerned glance with Nickie, then narrowed her eyes. "Why?"

"Well...because now the Gorafrex knows we're destroying them." Emily's smile came out as an apologetic grimace.

The tension erupting in Laura's shoulders made her entire body ache. "Please tell me you're just guessing, Em."

"No. I'm absolutely positive. It was there last night. In its new host."

"Oh, my *god.*" Laura set her coffee cup down on the table, splashing some of it, and stared at her youngest sister. "You went back there by yourself, without telling either of us, *and* you saw the Gorafrex?"

"Yeah."

"And you thought it was a good idea to wait until we woke up on our own before saying anything?"

Emily shrugged. "I mean, that's why I couldn't sleep…"

Nickie blinked and felt a little dizzy. "What happened, Em?"

"Well, it was seriously pissed that the energy core was broken. Win for the Hadstrom sisters. Then it saw me."

"Is that a guess," Laura asked, "or are you sure?"

"No, it definitely saw me. Right before it came after me."

Laura clenched her eyes shut. "*Please* tell me you didn't try to fight that thing by yourself, Em."

"I'm not stupid." Emily stared at her sisters, then tilted her head. "Okay, maybe a little reckless, yeah. But I didn't know it would show up at the same time. And, of course, I didn't try to fight it. I grabbed the socket wrench and popped out of there."

"And now it knows we're the ones destroying the energy cores," Nickie said.

"Probably, yeah. But that's not the most important thing." Emily swallowed. "The Gorafrex came after me, and it tried to do the whole drum-luring thing."

Laura opened her eyes and frowned. "What do you mean it *tried*?"

"I mean it tried. And the drums cut out after a few seconds." Emily glanced at Nickie, who stared at her with wide eyes, looking paler. "You okay?"

"Keep going," Nickie muttered.

"Okay. So, the drums wouldn't work, or whatever. It tried again and stopped again, like it couldn't...I don't know. Like a car engine that won't turn over, right? It was super pissed, as far as I could tell from the woman's face. And it yelled at me that it wasn't finished. Oh, that little shimmery thing happened again."

"What shimmery—"

"Like the first host. The guy in the vest. We chased him into the parking lot, remember? Then he kinda dropped, and the Gorafrex shimmered out of him."

Nickie nodded. "Before it took that woman as the next host."

"Right. That happened again last night. But the thing just, I dunno, sucked itself back into her body? And then it didn't seem to have any problem at all with the drums."

"It's getting stronger," Laura murmured, staring into her coffee cup.

"Yeah, I think so." Emily nodded. "I don't know how many hosts it's had since we found the...dead witch in the second host's house, but if the woman I saw last night was only the third, that means it's staying *inside* them longer."

"How'd you get away from it?" Nickie asked.

"The Clubhouse."

Nickie's eyes widened more. "What time was that?"

"I dunno. Maybe twelve-thirty. Almost one?"

"Oh, my god." Nickie buried her face in her hands and took a breath. "I should've come looking for you. I should've gone straight home, and if I knew you were gone, maybe I could've helped."

Emily blinked. "Really, Nickie. I'm okay."

"*Now* you're okay, yeah. But you almost weren't." Nickie shook her head and stared at the table. She took a sip of coffee to steel herself. "Okay, now *I* have to admit something."

Laura scoffed. "No way you went back to the energy core too."

"No. It's more like admitting to *not* doing something." Nickie bit her lip. "I should've told you guys about it Friday night at the show, but I didn't want you to start worrying for no reason, because it stopped. I thought maybe it was just a fluke or something."

Both sisters stared at her. All of Emily's bubbling, wired energy deflated when she put the pieces together. "You *did* hear the drums at the end of your show, didn't you?"

Nickie nodded. "And I heard them last night too."

CHAPTER TWENTY-FIVE

Nickie told them everything—hearing the Gorafrex's stunted drumbeat after her show; what their dad had told her about music *being* magic and how she had to learn to control it; the drumming returning again in short bursts at Ronnie's party; and having to pull over when they returned full force before she slipped into the Clubhouse to get away. When she finished, she felt better than she'd thought she would. *I know I have to keep lying to Chuck, but not to my sisters. Definitely didn't know it would feel this good to get it all out there.*

"Wait." Emily leaned over the table. "You must've showed up at the Clubhouse right after I left."

"I think so, yeah."

"And you didn't wonder why the giant socket wrench was there on the futon?"

Nickie frowned. "I don't think I was capable of noticing anything, Em. Why'd you leave it there?"

Emily shrugged. "I was gonna surprise Laura with it.

Like a present." She turned toward their oldest sister and grinned. "Surprise."

Nickie snorted, and Laura just shook her head. "I appreciate you thinking about me, Em. But I'm kinda having a hard time finding anything funny right now."

"Yeah…"

"Granted, I didn't think about how powerful the wrench is. Rutilda just gave it to me and said it would help, so it's good we have something we know can do serious damage to the energy cores."

"*And* we know what the Gorafrex's host looks like," Emily added with a nod. "Assuming it stays there much longer. That's a plus."

"Yep." Laura sighed. "But you shouldn't have gone back there by yourself. If that thing had gotten you…"

"But it didn't. I made it out just fine."

"You don't think that any of the things you've told us makes it okay that you disappeared, without telling us, and put yourself in that much danger, do you?"

Emily blinked and sat back in the chair. "No, Laura. Just tryin' to stay positive."

"Good. Stay positive. Just don't do it again, okay?"

Emily nodded.

Laura turned toward Nickie. "And *you* should've told us about the drums Friday night. As soon as you walked off that stage, Nickie. We need to *know* these things."

"Got it."

"You promised you'd tell us whenever they came back. Any little sound. Any sign of another headache that you couldn't be absolutely sure wasn't *just* a headache."

Nickie pressed her lips together. "I know. I promise I won't keep anything else from you guys."

"*Anything.*" Laura raised her eyebrows.

"Promise."

"Good. 'Cause, obviously, none of us can do this alone, and we definitely won't be able to do it if we're not together. That means no more secrets or lies just because we don't wanna freak each other out."

"Deal."

Emily nodded. "Yep. Deal."

"Okay." Laura sighed and absently wiped coffee stain off the rim of her mug and set it down. "I think the airport is the next energy core to get to. That's the other one with the most traffic and the most options for the Gorafrex to… switch hosts." Her sisters nodded. "Today."

Emily blinked. "Laura, I have to leave for work in fifteen minutes."

"Seriously?" The oldest Hadstrom sister spread her arms and frowned. "That thing knows what we're up to now, Em. That's obviously a lot more important than making one shift at your restaurant job."

Nickie sucked in a sharp breath through her teeth. *Uh-oh.*

Emily stood. "Okay…" She scooted the chair in behind her and nodded. "First of all, it's not just a restaurant job. It's actually the best step I've taken in my *career*, Laura."

"You know what I mean."

"Not really, no. 'Cause I'm pretty sure if you had some presentation to give or a class to teach or some…rare and unusual magical artifact to go dig up out of who knows where, you'd be asking us to wait until you were done. And you'd let us have it if we even *suggested* you put down your work or hire a temp or step away from *your* career so all three of us can go finish this thing that *you* started."

"Wait a minute, Em—"

"Nope. Sorry. You can wait a few more hours. When we hit all these energy cores and lock the Gorafrex up again —'cause I know we will—all of us will still have a life to go back to. I've already given up too many things for this *restaurant job* to throw away the best opportunity I have." Emily leaned toward her oldest sister, picked up Laura's mug, and took a long drink. "My shift's over at three. Maybe four. Text me where you want to meet."

"Emily, wait." Laura turned in her chair as her sister stalked through the living room toward the foyer. "Hey, I didn't mean it like that. I'm—"

The front door closed with a soft click.

"Sorry," Laura finished. She turned back to the table and closed her eyes. "I screwed that up, didn't I?"

"Uh…just a little bit, yeah." Nickie took a slow sip of coffee.

"You see where I'm coming from, though, right? I mean, it's not an outrageous request, given the circumstances."

Nickie shrugged. "Honestly, you both made valid points. And you're both right. We just hafta make room for both of you to be right."

"How?" Laura glanced at her with a concerned frown. "It's not like the Gorafrex is gonna wait for our schedules to open up."

"Compromise. Working around what we can do and what we *need* to do." Nickie tilted her head. "She'll go to work and blow off all that steam. Hopefully she eats something. And until her shift's over, you and I can work on what we need to work on before we go destroy some ancient Valikan technology tonight. Together."

Despite her frustration, Laura chuckled. "Destroy some ancient Valikan technology. That actually made me cringe."

"Kinda hurts your soul, huh?" Nickie nodded, and when she smirked, they both laughed for a bit.

"All right. I'm gonna go see if I can pinpoint where that energy core is under the airport. More or less."

"Good thing you're better at mapping stuff out than Dad, huh?"

"Yeah. *Really* good. Maybe I can figure out how that socket wrench works too. Seeing as I've got a few hours, apparently." Laura stood from the table and pushed her chair in. "What do you have goin' on today?"

"Nothing until Emily's off work." Nickie shrugged. "Actually, I think I'm gonna try what Dad told me last night. You know, playing music like it's an actual spell instead. Just in case we end up running into that thing again."

Laura nodded and headed into the dining room. Then she turned and added, "Just as long as you don't try to practice with Dad's lullaby, okay?"

Nickie blinked and shook her head. "Why not?"

"What? Come on..."

"I'm kidding." Nickie tossed her hand at her older sister, urging her to go do what she had to do. "Totally kidding."

Laura's chuckle was a little tense, and she eyed Nickie for a few seconds before slowly turning around. "Okay. I'll be upstairs."

"Got it."

The staircase creaked under Laura's footsteps as she headed up to her room. Nickie turned toward her cup of coffee for another long, slurping sip. "And I'll be down here learning how to master the guitar. Again."

CHAPTER TWENTY-SIX

Emily pulled into the Meadowlark Tavern's back lot fifteen minutes before her shift started. "I still can't believe she called this a *restaurant job*." She unbuckled her seatbelt and grabbed her chef's jacket from the passenger seat. "I literally just graduated college. She *knows* how much this means to me. And it's not any less than her *teaching job* means to her."

She stepped out of her car and shut the door a little harder than she meant to. "Great. Now I'm gonna have to work extra hard not to let any of this slip into the food and make everyone in the dining room all bent out of shape about their sister laughing at their dreams." Stuffing her arms into her chef's jacket, she turned around and stopped.

John stood there with his hands in his pockets, grinning beneath a small, confused frown. "That definitely wouldn't make the dinner guests very happy, would it?" He chuckled. "You know, I like the way you think, Emily. Good thing that's not actually possible."

If he only knew... She tried to hide her surprise behind a smile. "Uh…hello to you too."

"Oh, yeah. Hello." John tilted his head and walked toward her.

"What are you doing here?" Emily stuffed her keys into her back pocket and patted the other one to feel her phone still there. "I thought servers didn't come on 'til eleven."

"We don't."

"Okay…but it's eight o'clock in the morning."

He stopped about a foot away and smiled at her. "I just felt like stopping by."

"Uh-huh."

"Okay, actually, I was hoping you'd show up early so I could say hi. To you, specifically. 'Cause I know I won't get to do that once you're on the line."

That's both creepy and really sweet. Emily grinned. "I don't usually get here this early. So perfect timing, then."

"Thank you." John spun around on the asphalt and kicked his leg out before walking with her toward the restaurant. "Hey, so I really, *really* had a good time on Friday. Wanted to tell you that too."

"You showed up to work three hours early to say hi and, 'Thanks for an awesome night'?" Emily smirked, and he laughed. "I'm pretty sure that's what texting's for."

"Yeah, but I don't get to see you in a text."

"True." *Where is he going with this? Feels like he's working up to something.* "I'm glad you had a good time. I did too. It's been a while since I've gone to one of Nickie's shows with someone who's actually excited to be there."

"What?" John laughed and scratched the back of his

head. "Isn't that why people buy tickets to go see her? 'Cause they're actually excited to be there?"

"Well, yeah. I just meant…"

"Oh, you meant going with someone *else*. Like a date." He looked up at her and raised his eyebrows.

Not really a good time to start the conversation about exes. There's never a good time for that. "Yep." Emily folded her arms. "I guess that's what I meant. But so you know, it's been a really long time since I've been to any show at all with someone else. Except my sisters."

"Naw, I'm not worried about it. I thought it was amazing. As long as you had fun, we're all good."

Emily cast him a sideways glance and grinned. "I did. I totally had fun."

"Good." They stopped beside the back door to the kitchen, and John leaned against the brick wall. "I know I could've texted this to you too, but that feels…not as awesome."

She laughed. "Okay…"

"I wanna take *you* out. On another date." He shrugged and glanced past her with a sheepish smile. "One where I'm not as nervous 'cause it's a date *and* I'm standing backstage to watch one of the best blues-rock guitarists from twenty feet away."

"Wow." Emily wiggled her eyebrows. "Didn't realize how much pressure I put you under."

"Yeah. It was a lot of pressure."

She licked the smirk off her lips and asked, "When?"

"What?"

"When do you wanna take *me* out? On another date."

"Oh." He laughed and closed his eyes.

Those are the longest eyelashes I've ever seen on a guy. Didn't know I was into that until right now.

John looked at her and cocked his head. "How 'bout tonight?"

Emily wrinkled her nose. *There's no way in hell Laura's gonna be okay with pushing back this energy-core hunt so I can have a date. Probably not a good idea to even try.* "Tonight…"

"Doesn't look like a good time, huh?"

She shook her head. "Sorry. Plans with my sisters."

"Oh, yeah? You guys do a lotta stuff together, huh?"

"We sure do." Emily nodded. *That's a pretty new thing since we moved in together, actually.* "What about tomorrow?"

"Eh…" John grimaced and sucked in a breath through his teeth. "I'm closing tomorrow. Okay, if you tell me Tuesday's off the table, I'm gonna have to rethink my strategy here."

"Tuesday's good." She grinned at him. *Maybe by then we'll have the Gorafrex locked up with no more dead witches and no more awakened Peabrains running around.* "Let's go with Tuesday."

"Perfect. Third time's a charm, huh?" John ran a hand through his hair and sighed. "Is there anywhere you don't like to go? Just so I don't ruin my chances by planning something that turns out to be the worst idea ever."

Emily fought back a laugh. "Just as long as it's not underground, we're good."

He wrinkled his nose. "What?"

"Nothing. It's nothing. Just…an inside joke that, of course, you wouldn't get. Sorry."

"Okay. A club in a basement, though, that's still good?"

"Definitely."

"Cool." He studied her face a few seconds, then leaned toward her and shook his head. "It's not gonna be a club in a basement. Just so you know."

"Even if it was, we're all good." Emily laughed and tilted her head.

"Good to know. So, I'll just…call you before Tuesday and let you know where to meet? Or should I text you?"

"You could show up three hours early just to say hi and let me know."

That made him laugh, and he nodded. "Touché. Just so many options."

She raised her eyebrows. "You'll pick the right one."

His gaze steadied on hers, and his grin faded a little. "Yes, I will." He looked like he was about to say more. He turned to glance at the back door. "Right. I know you have to work, so I'll let you get to it."

"Okay."

"Okay." He kicked himself off the brick wall and stepped closer. "I know I'll still see you a few times before then, but now I'm just gonna be thinking about Tuesday."

"Oh, yeah?" Emily blinked up at him.

"Yeah. And you." John's gaze slid down to her lips. When Emily didn't pull away or say anything else, he finished what he started and kissed her.

His warm hand slid lightly against her cheek, and Emily kissed him back. Kissing John pushed everything else so far out of her head that by the time she realized she was just standing there with her arms at her sides, she also remembered she had to go to work. *Maybe I don't want to…* She set her hands lightly on his chest and pulled away.

John sighed and lowered his hand from her face. "Yeah, I know."

"I didn't say anything."

"But you still have to go to work. And we have the same boss, so…" He stepped away from her and shrugged. "I'm running the risk of getting us both in trouble."

Emily chuckled. "Definitely don't wanna get *you* in trouble."

Smirking, he took another step back and glanced at the door. "Well, too late for that. Just hasn't spread to my job, yet." He grinned and walked slowly backward across the parking lot. "Tuesday."

Oh, he's good. "Tuesday." Emily licked her lips, trying to keep from grinning like a lunatic, and forced herself to turn and open the door. She glanced back before she stepped inside to see him heading toward his truck.

He turned around to meet her gaze and smiled.

Really good. She chuckled and stepped into the kitchen.

CHAPTER TWENTY-SEVEN

After popping in and out of the Clubhouse, Laura sat at the desk in her bedroom, studying the Engineer's socket wrench. "Okay, if I'd found you tucked away under a boulder somewhere, the only thing I'd wonder is why anyone would make a wrench this huge." She rolled it over and examined the other side. "Nothing pins you as a magical artifact. Not even as a magical tool. Just one great, big hunk of metal shaped like a wrench that's probably spent the last couple million years underground with Rutilda. Unused. Forgotten." She chuckled. "Were you just lashing out when you knocked over the whole energy core?" One more time, she turned the wrench over and opened the top drawer of her desk. "As fun as that thought is, I don't think that's what happened." Laura reached for the magnifying glass in the drawer, then her phone vibrated on her desk and made her jump.

She snorted. "I thought vibrate mode was supposed to *keep* phones from scaring the crap out of their owners…"

She picked up her phone, recognized Nathan's number—though she hadn't saved it—and almost dropped it.

His text read: *'I know I said get back to me by four. Turns out the host of said party is wanting a head count.'*

"The party…" Laura sighed. "Totally forgot about that." She unlocked her phone and started a reply, then received another text.

'Also, I'm just really bad at being patient.' At the end of that one was a simple smiley face.

"Yeah, I can see that." She rolled her eyes and typed: *'I'm sorry, Nathan. I won't be able to make it tonight but thank you for inviting me.'*

The minute she sent it, the three dots in the bottom corner blinked to life. He sent a sad-face emoji, followed by: *'You sure?'*

"What? If I wasn't *sure*, I wouldn't have said it. That's—" She huffed and started to text back, but he beat her again.

'I really think you'd love it. Big old house right in Circle Ranch.'

"Oh, why? 'Cause every woman's supposed to be drawn in by a big old house in a super nice—wait. Where did I see that name?" Laura ran her hand over the papers on her desk and slipped out the rendition of the magical energy core map she'd copied to have in physical form. "No. That's too small." She snatched up her phone and tried not to punch her finger against the touch-screen keyboard.

'What's the address?'

Nathan sent back just as quickly, and she pulled up the map app on her phone. "No way." She zoomed out until the area of the map on her phone was the same as the circular one she'd drawn around the printed map of Austin. Laura blinked. "So…a part-Kashgar professor invited me to a party in the same neighborhood as one of the energy cores…" A wild, disbelieving laugh escaped her. "Unbelievable. I can't decide if that's a good thing or a bad thing." Sitting back in her desk chair, she clicked her tongue a few times and figured she might as well go for it.

She texted: *'Can my sisters come?'*

'Depends on how many sisters you have.'

Laura rolled her eyes. "Very cute."

'Just two.'

'Bring your sisters!'

"And…I told Nickie I'd ask about plus-ones, didn't I?" Shaking her head, Laura sent him yet another question: *'Can they bring dates?'*

'For sure. You can't, though.'

Laura snorted. "So he went from, 'Yeah, bring your sisters,' to incredibly rude in less than thirty seconds? What is *wrong* with this—"

Nathan's next text came through. *'Because I'll already be there.'* Punctuated with a winking emoji.

"He literally just…oh, my god. He called this a date and made it the worst joke ever at the same time." The confusing part was she had no idea how she felt about it. The only thing she *could* do was laugh.

'Okay. We'll be there. Five of us.'

Nathan's final reply was a lot simpler than his previous enthusiasm.

'6:00 p.m. Can't wait.' After that was a grinning emoji, and the conversation was apparently over.

"Not like anybody can really express very much through a text." Laura squinted at the screen. "And a grinning emoji." She shook her head, checked the screen one more time, and grinned. "Guess we're going to a party. And no one else needs to know that we're doing it only to get right up close and personal with another energy core. Because those *definitely* need to go first." That thought brought her unexpected giddiness down a notch and replaced it with her usual Laura Hadstrom brand of determination. "That's more like it."

She glanced at the map of Austin on her desk and all twelve points where they'd find the energy cores. She'd highlighted the intersection at the Thinkery in yellow. "Guess I should tell Nickie and Emily and start getting ready for what'll probably be the weirdest night ever…"

Her gaze fell to her phone again, and she snatched it up for one more text. "I can't believe I didn't think about this. Wait…is it against some kinda rule to text right after making plans like that? I don't even know how to—no. Laura, stop it." She pointed at her phone and scowled. "You're doing this for the energy core first. Probably also to protect people. Maybe a little bit as a…" She swallowed. "Date. That's the least important part."

She typed and sent the text before she could change her mind: *'Is this a magicals-only kind of party?'*

The little dots while Nathan typed flashed on her screen, disappeared, and repeated that back and forth until Laura wanted to toss her phone across the room. Finally, he sent a reply.

'I definitely had another witty response to that, but I think I've reached my quota for cheeseball jokes. Not strictly magicals, no. Maybe half and half. Does that kill it for you?'

Laura scoffed. "Oh, please. Don't be so dramatic."

'No. My sisters' dates are human. I just wanted to make sure.'
'All good. See you at 6:00!'

"Okay, now that looks like an official end to conversation, Laura. You're done." She shoved her phone into her back pocket and took another look at the map. "And we're gonna have to keep this hidden from everybody. Real fun night."

With a nod, she glanced around her room and found herself feeling remarkably satisfied by the serendipity of getting to hit up Nathan's party and another energy core at the same time. "Literally." She smirked and walked out of her room.

She found Nickie downstairs in the living room with her Strat in hand and the strap over her head and shoulder. Nickie had just finished plugging in the cables when she rounded the corner. "How's it comin along in here for you—"

Nickie struck a blaring chord, and the amp roared with electric guitar. The force of it made Laura stop dead in her tracks, feeling the vibrations through the floor and halfway up her legs before Nickie clamped a hand down on the strings.

"Woah. Sorry." Her sister smirked. "Goin' pretty well in here, actually. I think. Kind of amazing how one little tweak in mindset can change the whole freakin' picture. Wanna see?"

"Yeah…but you gotta turn that down first."

"Right." Nickie lowered the amp's volume, then stood behind the couch. "Okay. I know it's really not much, but it's better than nothing. And I've only been at it for like, I dunno, a couple hours? Just…okay. Just watch." She bent down to pick a tissue off the floor and set it on the back of the couch.

Laura folded her arms. "Um…"

"I know. Just bear with me." Nickie gave the Strat an experimental strum, and when she looked at her older sister to check about the noise, Laura nodded.

Then Nickie started playing. It could have been a solo—and probably was—starting out fast and light and almost fluttering. Nickie closed her eyes a few seconds, fingers on the fretboard and her lime-green pick moving faster and faster. When her eyes flew open, Laura thought she saw a dark flash from the black legacy ring on her sister's thumb. She wasn't sure because her attention was diverted to the tissue on the back of the couch.

It was trembling.

Just a little at first, as if someone had turned on a box fan at the other side of the room. Then, the thin paper flapped wildly, fluttering as quickly as Nickie's fingers shredded the devious solo. When the tissue lifted into the air inch by wavering inch, it could no longer be mistaken for a tissue buffeted by a fan. The white paper didn't blow off the couch or across the room but lifted straight up, higher and higher, until it hung suspended in the center of the living room, flapping wildly. Nickie's fingers moved faster than Laura could follow them, lips twitching with intense concentration as she stared at the floating tissue. With a squealing slide and a final chord, Nickie stopped, and the tissue floated down to land on a seat cushion.

"No way…" Laura whispered. She stared at the tissue, then glanced at her sister. "No *way.*"

"I know." Nickie wiped beads of sweat from her forehead, breathing heavily. "Pretty insane, right?"

"Yeah, that's one way of putting it." Laura cocked her head. "You can cast a levitating spell on stuff just by playing a song?"

"Well, just the tissue so far." Nickie shrugged and pulled the guitar strap over her head and set the Strat in its stand. "It's kinda ridiculous. I feel like I'm ten again and waving my wand around for the first time. I don't know if it's just 'cause I like the Strat better, or because it's louder, or... maybe just because having music blasting out of something helps me focus." She chuckled. "But I think I got it to go a little higher this time." Tossing her hair back, she took a deep breath. "Definitely a step in the right direction."

"Yep. That's definitely what that is. And Dad knew this would happen when you told all that stuff about music *being* magic?"

"Uh...I don't think so." Nickie folded her arms and shook her head. "I mean, he definitely put the idea in my head. I wouldn't have figured this out without him. But I don't think he knew what was really possible. I mean, unless you remember him casting spells with his guitar when we were kids."

Laura laughed. "I would definitely remember that."

"Yeah, me too."

"You think you have enough of a handle on it to play the lullaby?" Laura licked her lips. "You know, if we happen to run into the Gorafrex again at the next energy core?"

"I mean, I can't exactly practice with the lullaby to really know. We don't need that thing showing up at our house just because I wanna test out my new skills." Nickie snorted. "But yeah. Yeah, I think I have enough of a handle on it. At least enough not to play myself into a coma again."

"Good." The oldest Hadstrom sister nodded, eyed the tissue on the couch again, and grinned. "So…we're going to that party tonight."

"Really? I thought you were pretty gung-ho about going for the energy core at the airport."

"Well, I was." Laura shrugged. "Turns out the party's in the same neighborhood, so it's actually a good opportunity. We can be there and take a look around without anyone wondering what the heck we're doing, and…well, Nathan said it's a mixed-bag party, right? Magicals and humans. We have to be careful, but we can at least be there to make sure everyone's okay after the energy core's smashed."

Nickie chuckled. "Don't forget about the fun, Laura."

"What?"

"It's a *party*. Which is also a good opportunity to have fun. Let loose for just a few minutes, even. You remember how to do that, right?"

"Do I—of *course* I remember how to have fun. I can be fun." Laura shot her sister a dubious frown. "Unless you wanna make the whole thing un-fun. We can just go to the airport energy core instead."

"Oh, come on. Who picks the airport over a party?"

Laura smirked. "That's what I thought. Invite Chuck, if you want. Got the okay for that too."

"Excellent." Nickie grinned. "This'll totally be fun."

"Just don't let your expectations get too high, okay? We'll still be there for a pretty important reason."

"Yeah, no problem."

Laura took out her phone. "I'm gonna text Emily to let

her know, and then we need to grab everything we have and make sure we bring it—oh." Her eyes widened, and a grin slowly spread across her lips.

"Okay, it's really creepy when you smile that way."

"Not creepy. Just seriously awesome." She finished the text to Emily, sent it, and stuck her phone back in her pocket. "I think I know how to make it up to Emily after this morning."

"You mean after you belittled her career by calling it meaningless?"

"Stop it." Laura rolled her eyes. "But yeah. To make up for that. Like a peace offering."

Nickie chuckled. "Do I wanna know what that is, or…"

"You'll see it when she does. I'm gonna go get started on that. Can you…" Laura glanced behind her and across the foyer at the dining room table with the lance and one of Emily's iron spheres on it. "Can you put those in the Clubhouse? And whatever else you think might be a good energy-core-destroyer?"

"You're gonna use the Clubhouse as a giant purse, aren't you?"

Laura laughed and headed toward the stairs. "You know, that's a ridiculous analogy, but yeah. A giant weapon purse. Something for every occasion, right?"

Nickie laughed as her older sister bounded up the stairs.

CHAPTER TWENTY-EIGHT

Emily moved through her work on the line in a fog. She couldn't stop thinking about John and the way he'd kissed her in the parking lot. *Not that the rear lot is the most romantic place or anything. And not that I'm the most romantic person. Guess it doesn't matter when he somehow always says the right thing and kisses me like* that...

"Hadstrom!" Chef Ansler's growling shout pulled her out of the fog, and she realized it wasn't the first time he'd shouted for her.

"Sorry. I mean, yes, Chef."

"What is *up* with you tonight?" Meadowlark's Head Chef moved toward the back of the kitchen past the sauté and fry stations and stopped in front of her at the soup station. "You feelin' okay?"

"Yes, chef."

"Drop the salute, Hadstrom. I'm serious. You look flushed and glassy-eyed." He scrutinized her with a skeptical frown. "You get high before stepping into my kitchen?"

"What? No, Chef." His frown darkened, and she shook her head. "Sorry. No."

"Would you take a drug test right now?"

"With an hour left in my shift and orders still coming in?"

Chef Ansler's eyes narrowed so much, he might as well have closed them. The man was sweaty and critical, but he was also concerned. "Yeah. Right now."

Emily puffed out a breath, gestured toward the order line, and shrugged. "I mean, yeah. If you don't trust me and you don't mind the soup orders getting backed up, sure. I'll take a drug test."

"Good. Stay here." He walked toward the front of the kitchen bustling with the other chefs at their stations, all working to run the well-oiled machine that was Meadowlark.

"Wait, so do you want me to or not?" Emily called after him.

"No, I trust you." The Head Chef turned around and spread his arms. "I just want you to do your job, Hadstrom."

"Yes, Chef." She went back to stirring the chicken soup with jasmine rice, summer squash, and lima beans she'd made in a daze that morning and now kept hot—but not too hot—on the stove. "Jeeze," she muttered. "The mind games and this guy. I don't even *get* high." She shook her head and frowned at the soup.

The minute her mind turned back to John, the kitchen door burst open, and John actually came storming into the kitchen. "I don't think I can do this again."

Another server in her mid-thirties dashed into the

kitchen behind him. "John, come on. We still need you out there."

"I don't know if it's this place or some kinda full-moon thing twice in two weeks, but this is nuts." He threw his arms up and turned to face the other server. "Those people are crazy, Annie. Did you see what she did?"

"Yeah." Annie swallowed. "I think she was just trying to be friendly—"

"That wasn't friendly." He jerked a hand toward the kitchen door. "She practically *molested* me! Like just randomly, out of the blue, tried to jump my bones."

Emily froze. "What the hell…"

"That crap's not supposed to happen at *all*, let alone in a place like this." John smoothed his hair away from his forehead with both hands. "Unless you have a better way to handle how freaked out I am right now, just give me a minute, okay?"

"John, we're fully sat—"

"Yeah, I know. I know. Don't worry about my tables. I'll get to them. Go do your thing."

The server frowned, then jumped a little when she remembered something else important and stepped through the kitchen. "Chef Ansler?"

The Head Chef turned around and raised his eyebrows at her. "Yeah."

"Um…the woman at fourteen's been asking to speak to you for the last fifteen minutes."

"The same one?"

Annie nodded.

"Did you explain to her we're working a full line back here?"

"Multiple times, yeah." The server bit her lip. "She's really adamant about it, Chef. Said she'd…" She leaned toward Chef Ansler but still had to raise her voice to be heard over the clink and hiss and spitfire communication in the kitchen. "…call her husband and tell him everything if you don't come out in the next two minutes."

Chef Ansler leaned away from her, blinked, and shook his head. "What the hell is wrong with these people?" He stalked around Annie and pushed open the swinging kitchen door with an aggravated shove. The server turned in a small circle, glanced at all the chefs—who pretended they hadn't noticed—then dashed back out into the dining room.

Emily turned off the burner beneath the soup pot and wiped her hands on a dry rag. John moved down the side of the kitchen toward the back. When he met her gaze, he shook his head, then disappeared into the staff room. Emily took her chances going after him.

He was sitting in one of the chairs against the wall when she stopped in the doorway. "Hey. What's going on?"

"I have no idea." He was bent over, forearms on his thighs, shaking his head as one knee bounced up and down in agitation. His wide-eyed gaze settled on the staff room floor, and he didn't look up.

Emily bit her lip. "I, uh…heard you talking to Annie just now. Something about a woman at one of your tables…"

John winced and shook his head. "Yeah, she was just… she was really grabby, like, in the weirdest way ever." He sighed and rubbed his face. "Feels just like the other night, right? Like a week ago. When everyone out there started climbing up on the tables and shouting about how they were the best at whatever and completely losing their shit."

"Uh-oh..." Emily bit her lip and couldn't think of a single thing to say. *I seriously screwed up again, didn't I?*

John scoffed. "Yeah, *big* uh-oh." He glanced up at her, as if he hadn't meant to say it out loud and closed his eyes. "Sorry, Emily. I'm just...it was weird last week, and it's really freakin' weird again, and it feels like the whole world's going crazy."

More like head-over-heels crazy, I bet. And only the people who ate my soup. Man, I really need to pay more attention to what I'm doing. The only thing she could think of to say was, "Yeah, I bet."

John puffed out a sigh and shook his head. "I really need a cigarette."

Okay, how did I forget that one unappealing detail? She leaned back and glanced at the kitchen. "Go take a smoke break."

He looked at her and blinked. "No. I quit. No more smokes for me."

"Really?" Emily tilted her head and studied him. "When?"

"Uh...Thursday night." He let out a humorless chuckle and nodded, trying to convince himself he still agreed with that decision. "Well, that was the last one. I really only smoke at work. And Friday when I came in, you invited me to Nickie's show. I could tell how much you don't like it, and I like you a lot more, so...I'm done."

Okay, admittedly, I'm a little flattered.

Shaking his head, he shrugged. "It was actually goin'

pretty well until all this craziness. Did you see what's goin' on out there?"

Emily swallowed. "Nope." *But I'm pretty sure we can blame the whole thing on me thinking about that kiss while I was cooking...* "You know, I think it's probably just a—"

The kitchen door burst open so hard it smacked the kitchen wall with a *thud* before swinging closed again.

"She's an insane person!" Chef Ansler stormed into the kitchen with Annie on his heels. "Apparently, my restaurant is a goddamn looney bin!" He slammed a hand down on the order line and started pacing. "We managed to get things back under control last week with that...that weird...whatever the hell happened, nobody said a word. But half the people out there have lost their minds, and I'm gonna be all over the goddamn news as the five-star chef whose running a...a freakin' *whorehouse*. And it's three fifteen in the afternoon!"

"Oh, boy." Emily groaned and looked at John. "I'm gonna go see if there's anything I can do."

He smirked. "You don't happen to have any more of that mushroom soup, do you? Seemed to calm people down the last time."

"Uh...yeah, that was a one-time thing." She wrinkled her nose. "I don't think this is the same situation."

"Only in how nuts it is." He nodded at her. "If anyone asks, just tell them I'll be out in two minutes."

"Sure."

"Thanks, Em."

Hearing him use her nickname made her stop and look at him.

John held her gaze even as his foot kept pumping up

and down on the floor, and his small smile was both apologetic and grateful.

"No problem." She smiled, winked, and headed into the kitchen.

Chef Ansler had moved to the other side of the kitchen by the second walk-in, rubbing his fingers over his lips as he scowled and listened to both Annie and his Sous Chef talk to him at the same time. The other chefs at their stations and on the line kept working to complete the waiting orders, but they'd slowed down enough to do their jobs and sneak occasional glances at their boss.

Emily made a straight line toward the kitchen door and stopped to peer through the window into the dining room. Her eyes grew wide, and she took in a long, slow breath. "Oh, yeah. I seriously screwed up again."

Everything John and Chef Ansler said made perfect sense now. At the table closest to the kitchen, a woman in her seventies sat on the lap of a man barely into his thirties, twirling her fingers in his hair and whispering in his ear as he stroked her thigh. A couple who might have been eating their meal together were now definitely enjoying each other's company, making out like crazy beside their table before the man swept their entire dinner onto the floor with his arm and lowered her onto the tabletop.

A woman squealed and darted across the dining room. Emily was about to burst out of the kitchen to come help her before she realized her squeal was actually a laugh. The man chasing the woman was laughing too, wiggling his fingers at her until she stopped, spun around, and pressed her back against the restaurant wall to shoot him a simpering glance. The minute he reached her, they gripped each other fiercely and fumbled with each other's clothing.

Tables joined other tables in sitting on laps, kissing strangers, whispering sweet-and-spicy nothings into their neighbors' ears. The sounds of laughter, kissing, and a few moans from somewhere Emily didn't even want to see rose through the kitchen door. The last of the guests who *hadn't* ordered the chicken soup rose quickly from their table when a necktie and a pair of pantyhose came sailing from the other end of the dining room to land on the center-piece. The couple hurried out the front door, casting disgusted and fearful looks behind them.

Emily clamped a hand over her mouth and spun away from the kitchen door. *I have no idea how to fix this. I don't even know* how *to fix this.* She dragged her hand down her lips and over her chin. "Just get back to work," she muttered. "It'll run its course. It always does. Yeah." With a nod, she headed to her soup station and pretended to forget everything she'd just seen—just like the rest of the chefs.

She reached out to turn the burner back on beneath the soup, then stopped. *And keep this thing going? No, thanks.* Instead, she took advantage of all the other chefs focusing so hard on trying to focus and dumped the rest of her chicken-and-orgy soup into the trashcan beside her station. "Eighty-six chicken soup," she shouted. The other chefs echoed their confirmation back at her without missing a beat at their own stations. Emily took the pot and the lid to the industrial sink beside the dishwasher and left it there.

On her way back, she saw John stepping out of the staff

room. He smiled at her as he headed through the kitchen, looking a lot more in control of himself now. She lifted her hand and crossed her fingers, which made him roll his eyes and laugh before he pushed through the swinging kitchen door.

She was scheduled to work until 4:00 p.m., and the second she saw the clock over the swinging door reach 4:00 p.m., she stepped around her sprayed, scrubbed, and dried-spotless station.

Chef Martino glanced over from where he diced onions at the sauté station. "What are you doing?" he asked.

Emily glanced at Chef Ansler still fuming against the far wall. "I'm scheduled 'til four…"

"Then get outta here."

"Are you sure it's—"

"Yep." He smirked, shook his head, and went back to dicing. "Nobody's staying here later than they have to tonight. Trust me."

"Okay. Thanks."

Chef Martino puffed out a breath, rolled his eyes, and kept chopping.

Emily went to the staff room and shrugged out of her chef's coat. Her car keys and phone went from her locker to her back pockets, and she paused. "I hope John's okay out there. Maybe I should—" She shook her head. "No. He's working. And I don't think I'd step into that dining room right now if someone offered me a million bucks." Folding her chef's coat over her arm, she left the staff room to head for the kitchen's back door.

She gave a final glance at the kitchen. All the orders had gone out, and most of the chefs were keeping busy with a head start on tomorrow's prep work or cleaning up their stations or trying not to look like they waited for Chef Ansler to explain the seriously freaky day in his restaurant. *Looks like things are settling down a little. Yeah, I knew they would.* Pressing her lips together, she walked outside into the parking lot.

Once she got behind the wheel of her Honda Civic and started it up, she pulled out her phone and found a text from Laura.

'Going to that party after all. Energy core in the same neighborhood. If you don't have time to come home first, meet us there at 6:00. You can bring John.' Below that was an address.

Emily shook her head. "I can bring John. Awesome. Still not an apology, Laura." She glanced at the seat behind her and nodded. "Got a change of clothes in the car and one iron-orb…weapon at the Clubhouse. Think I'm pretty good to go."

She cocked her head and typed out a reply: *I'll meet you there.'*

Then, just because she knew it would make her feel better, at least, she pulled up her text thread with John.

'Party tonight? Turns out it's not just a sister thing. And this doesn't let you off the hook for Tuesday.' She copied the address into another text and sent that too.

Then she took a deep breath, shifted into drive, and left Meadowlark Tavern to spend a few hours somewhere quiet, by herself, without any distractions. "I hope."

CHAPTER TWENTY-NINE

"There she is." Laura nodded at the slate-gray Honda coming down the street. Nickie and Chuck stopped on their way up the driveway to turn around and look. "You think she's still mad at me?"

Nickie shrugged. "You'll know in a minute."

"What happened?" Chuck asked.

"Laura crapped all over Emily's aspirations to be a chef. No big deal."

"Woah."

"That's a really crude way to put it, Nickie." Laura frowned at her sister. "And I realize I should've paid more attention to the way I phrased things."

"Yep."

"Okay." Chuck lifted both hands and smirked. "I'm not gonna ask any more about it."

"Well, thanks, Chuck." Laura barely cracked a smile as she watched Emily get out of her car and walk across the street toward them. The second her sister stepped onto the driveway, Laura spread her arms. "Hey, glad you made it. Is John coming?"

"After his shift, yeah." Emily didn't meet her gaze.

"How was yours?"

Emily shot Laura a blank stare. Then she blinked and headed for the front door. "I need a drink."

"Right there with ya, Em." Chuck hurried after her.

Nickie glanced at Laura. "Maybe she'll like your present. And apology."

"She's gotta let me give them to her first." They followed Emily and Chuck up to the front porch and stopped just before the front door opened.

"Hi…" A witch in her mid-thirties with short, bright-red hair and wearing a lavender romper grinned at them. "I'm Vanessa." She stuck out her hand to shake each of theirs, and they introduced themselves.

Laura was the last to do so, and when she told the woman her name, Vanessa's eyes widened. "Oh, *you're* Laura. Nathan hasn't stopped talking about you since he got here."

That's not weird. Laura smiled. "I know we're a little late, but he told me the party started at six."

"Oh, you're fine. He just got here *really* early." Vanessa chuckled and stepped aside. "Come on in."

They all stepped into the large, elegantly decorated house. Laura appreciated the theme followed decorative patterns from the American Southwest in pastel colors. "I'll let Nathan know you're here." Vanessa turned and disappeared into the next room.

"There's an actual *bar* here." Chuck stared at them and

wiggled his eyebrows. "Built into the wall. Babe, you want anything?"

"Yeah. A beer? Whatever's good."

"You got it." He strolled off into what looked like the den, nodding and smiling and striking up casual conversation with the other people standing there as he headed for the bar.

"What kinda party did you say this was?" Nickie asked.

"Uh…he said it was a 'Welcome to Austin' party." Laura gazed at the oil paintings lining the entryway and shrugged. "I think most of these people are from his department."

"Oh, good. A bunch of physicists." Emily clapped her hands and rubbed them together. "This'll be so much fun."

Laura turned toward her sister. "You know, if you let yourself be just a little—"

"Hey." Nathan took a few jogging steps around the corner, then slowed as he approached them. "I wasn't sure if you'd actually show up. Glad you did." He grinned. "These your sisters?"

"Yeah." Laura gestured to each of them in turn. "Nickie and Emily. This is Nathan."

"Great to meet you guys. Hey, I'm gonna go make some drinks. Anybody want anything?"

"Vodka soda," Emily said curtly. "That would be awesome."

"Got it."

Nickie shook her head and nodded at the bar. "My order's already in. That blond guy playing superstar barista over there is Chuck."

Nathan laughed. "Glad he's got you covered. I'll go say hi. Laura?"

"Um…just a light beer, I guess?"

"No problem." He headed into the den and waved them forward. "Come on in. Get comfortable. I'll bring you your drinks."

"Thanks." Laura smiled, and the minute he turned around to face the bar, she whipped her head toward Emily. "I don't think it's such a good idea to start off with a vodka soda, Em. We have one thing to do here that's a little more important than drinking."

"Huh." Emily stared after Nathan and blinked. "I don't think you know what a dwarf is." She turned toward Laura and jerked her thumb back toward the bar. "'Cause that guy is definitely not a dwarf."

Nickie snorted. "Yeah, you had us goin' there for a minute. What is he really?"

Laura glanced between her sisters, then rolled her eyes. "We can have this conversation later. Right now, we're mingling. In a little bit, we're gonna find the energy core in this neighborhood and smash it to pieces." With a firm nod, Laura squared her shoulders and headed into the den, smiling when she saw Chuck and Nathan laughing behind the bar. *At least* someone's *having a good time at this thing.*

They didn't move farther than the den the first two hours. Nathan had no problem keeping everyone entertained with stories of his last teaching job in Ohio, and then he felt the need to switch to the topic to how he met Laura, starting with her holding the door open for him as he struggled with his stack of boxes. He did conveniently leave out the minor magical details of her blasting the drawer out of her desk and him *helping* her with it; Chuck wasn't the only human in the room who still didn't know magic existed.

Emily slowly sipped her vodka tonic until it was empty, and she'd considered making her another one for the last half hour. *Nathan definitely gets points for making a stiff drink. And Laura wasn't wrong about us having to stay on our game...*

Her phone vibrated in her back pocket, and just as one of the other guests delivered the punchline she'd only halfway paid attention to, she pulled up the text from John.

'Just got here. I think.'

The room exploded with laughter.

"Oh, thank god." Emily turned toward the entryway.

"Everything okay?" Nickie asked.

"It is now." Emily wrinkled her nose at her sister and struggled not to skip toward the front door. When she opened it, she found John walking up the sidewalk and frowning at his phone. "Hey!"

"Thanks for steppin' out." He grinned and headed up the driveway. "I really wasn't sure if this was the right place."

"Well, I don't know if it's the *right* place, but this is definitely the party."

He chuckled and slipped his hands into his pockets as Emily spun in a quick half-circle and walked with him back to the front door.

"Everything okay?" he asked.

"I dunno." She shrugged. "It's been a super weird day for everyone, I think."

"You can say that again."

"How did everything go after I left?"

John puffed out a sigh and shook his head. "It kinda just…worked itself out, I think. People eventually settled down. They all seemed really confused, but nobody wanted to admit it or apologize. Nobody talked about it at all. I *did* get a twenty-percent tip from the handsy lady, though."

"Well that's a plus." Emily smirked.

"I guess…Ansler was still pretty pissed when we closed down."

"He's always pissed."

John laughed, and they stepped inside together.

The conversation hushed soon as they rejoined Emily's sisters, Nathan, Chuck, and the half-dozen other friends and associates in the den. Nathan grinned and spread his arms. "Hey. John, right?"

"Yeah, hi."

The physics professor stuck out his hand. "Nathan." They shook, then Nathan took a sip of his liquor drink.

"He works with Laura," Emily added.

"We don't really work together." Laura shook her head with a quick laugh. "He teaches physics and happened to get the empty office across the hall from mine."

"Wow." Nathan grinned. "You really like to make sure there's no room for confusion, don't you?"

Laura opened her mouth and couldn't find anything to say.

John nodded with wide eyes and glanced at Emily. "Good stuff."

"Yup."

One of the women in the den with them leaned

forward and lifted a hand. "Excuse me for a minute. I haven't eaten anything, so I'm going to raid Vanessa's kitchen." A few people chuckled, and one of the men went with her.

Emily fought the urge to roll her eyes and shout for the actual party to get started. *I was hoping this wouldn't be a stuffy academic party. Guess that's what I get for hopin'.*

"Okay. I think I've talked everyone's ears off long enough. And…" Nathan peered around the corner toward the kitchen. "…I don't know where Vanessa went. Laura? Will you help me figure out how to get her sound system working?"

"Um…" Laura glanced at Nickie and Chuck, who both failed at offering inconspicuous nods. "Yeah, okay." She walked hesitantly toward him, and he led her across the den to a complicated-looking audio system.

John leaned toward Emily as he eyed the other people in the room with them. "This wasn't really the kind of party I was expecting."

"Oh, me, neither." She laughed. "Okay, so there's one thing I won't enjoy doing when we go out on Tuesday."

"What's that?"

"This."

They both laughed.

"Ah, but nice bar. Is it help yourself?" John asked.

"Yeah, definitely get a drink."

He grinned and headed off to do just that.

Emily turned to look at Laura and Nathan by the sound system. *Man, she's tense. Standing there like a plank. Way to make it super obvious you don't know how to talk to guys, Laura. If I didn't already know she'd get pissed at me, I'd go be her wingman right now.* She looked up at Nickie and Chad, who were both trying hard to look interested in what a middle-aged woman with hilariously magnifying bifocals was saying about String Theory. *Weirdest day ever.*

She saw Laura laugh, which was a good sign. Nathan said something else with animated gestures before a soft crackle filled the room, then the music started. *"There* we go," Nathan shouted and led her back toward the rest of the group. "If anyone has a problem with James Brown you can listen to something else. At your own house." A few people laughed, and Nathan leaned toward Laura to say something in her ear. Her eyes grew wide, and she shot him a sideways glance without saying anything.

"I think it's time to dance," Nickie said, grinning up at Chuck. Her boyfriend had already started with his less-than-ideal dance moves, which made her throw her head back and laugh. Then she was moving with him, spinning and stomping around the den. A few others joined in, and John returned to Emily with two beer bottles.

He handed her one and nodded at Nickie and Chuck. "I wanna go to *their* party."

Emily laughed. "If we stay here long enough, I think this'll *be* their party." She tipped her beer toward him, he tapped his against it, and they drank. Chuck spun in an awkward circle, flinging his hands in the air, and Emily almost sprayed beer out her nose.

"Come on, Em." John bobbed his head and moved his body to the rhythm. "I got to dance at a Nickie Hadstrom show with you. You can't pass up James Brown."

Emily took a long drink of her beer, raised an eyebrow at him, and moved her feet.

CHAPTER THIRTY

There was a lull in sound as the end of the last track faded. The woman who'd gone off into the kitchen to look for food used it as an opportunity to return to the den, blinking furiously and scanning the faces of everyone waiting to dance to the next song.

"Hey, has anyone seen Vanessa?"

Nobody said anything, but several turned and shook their heads.

"I'm just…I haven't seen her for a while, and I guess she didn't tell anyone where she was going."

"I haven't seen her since we got here," Chuck offered.

"Okay." The woman frowned. "I'm sorry, everybody. I just…she doesn't normally do this, so…" She glanced behind her into the kitchen and slid a hand across her forehead. "She won't answer her phone, either."

"I'm sure she's fine, Beth." Nathan turned the music down so they could hear better. "I mean, she knows there are a bunch of people having fun in her house. Maybe she just stepped out for a bit to get some air."

"Yeah." Beth blinked again and took a deep breath. "That sounds like something she'd do."

"Yeah. She'll be back." Nathan turned up the volume and shuffled toward the center of the den, taking Laura's hand and spinning her. Laura rolled her eyes, turning slowly with a barely touched beer in her hand, but she smiled.

Nickie grinned at Chuck as he wiggled around in front of her. *This guy dances like a toddler. Looks like Emily's finally enjoying herself.* Her sister and John cracked up over something only they could hear. Nickie smiled, and then a sharp, intense pressure flared behind her eyes. Three quick, blaring drumbeats followed. She sucked in a breath. *Really? Now?*

Swallowing, she lifted her beer bottle at Chuck and wiggled it. "I'm getting another one."

He nodded and kept dancing, and she headed straight for Laura. The minute Laura saw her, her smile disappeared.

Nathan cocked his head at her. "Everything okay?"

"I'm…not sure."

Nickie smiled quickly up at the very tall Nathan. "Hey, sorry to cut in. Laura, I'm startin' to get a—" Another burst of pain flared at her temple, followed by a burst of the Gorafrex's drums that lasted longer this time. Nickie closed her eyes and pushed through it. "I'm getting' a headache, I think. Feels like someone's pounding on my head with a *drum.*"

"Oh." Laura glanced at Nathan. "Oh, no. Do you need something for it?"

"Yeah, I could use your help."

"I'm sure Vanessa has something somewhere." Nathan spread his arms. "I'll go look."

"No, thanks." Laura patted his arm without looking away from her sister. "Nickie has to take this special kind of migraine medicine. Super hard to find."

Chuck stepped up behind her and lightly rubbed Nickie's back. "Super hard to find," he repeated and nodded at Nathan. "I've tried to find it; it's liking digging for buried treasure."

Nickie smiled at him. "Sorry, babe. I think I need to—" The drums started up again, this time without the building pressure as a warning. She hunched her shoulders and clenched her eyes shut, trying to breathe through it.

"Woah, it's that bad, huh?"

"Yeah. They come on fast." Laura caught Emily's gaze and waved her over. "Nickie's got a migraine," she said when both Emily and John joined them.

"One of the really bad ones?" Emily raised her eyebrows.

"Yeah, Em." Nickie gritted her teeth. "One of *those*."

"Okay, so let's go." Emily nodded at the front door and guided Nickie toward it with a hand on her sister's back.

"Uh…" John spread his arms. "You need any help, or—"

"Nope. We got it." Laura nodded and hurried out the door after her sisters.

The three men left at the party without their dates stared at the door none of the Hadstrom sisters had bothered to close behind them.

John cocked his head. "They do that a lot, don't they?"

Chuck nodded. "Oh, yeah."

With a frown, Nathan squinted and just said, "Huh."

The Hadstrom sisters hurried down the neighborhood sidewalk. Emily and Laura walked on either side of Nickie, supporting her as much as they could while trying to be quick. "Still happening?" Emily asked.

"Yeah." Nickie swallowed. "Off and on. You guys can hear it too, right?"

"It's getting louder." Laura stared down the street in the darkness, which was lit only by a few yellow pools from the streetlights. "We're going in the right direction, at least."

"Okay, so this has to mean the Gorafrex is here, right?" Emily tightened her grip on Nickie's arm when her sister stumbled. "Like it maybe has another witch or wizard, or it's at the energy core. Or both."

"Right now, I'd say that's the best assumption." The ancient, hastily beating drums came again, and Laura cocked her head. "Wait. That sounds like it's coming from —" She glanced into the street and rolled her eyes. "Again with the manholes?"

"How else do you get underground out here, Laura?" Emily helped Nickie down off the sidewalk, and they hurried toward the manhole cover in the middle of the street.

Laura pointed at the metal disk, her silver ring flashed, and the thing popped out a lot more gracefully than the first time. "That's an improvement." She stepped toward the gaping black hole in the asphalt and peered down.

Pointing, she dropped an orb of light down into the hole so they could see the bottom. "Faster with a transport bubble."

"Got it." Emily flicked her wrist, and a shimmering bubble grew from her ring until it was big enough for all three of them. "Belowground floor." She smirked, and her sisters stepped in with her.

The bubble popped two seconds later, and they looked up to see the night sky in the open ring above them. "Okay." Laura looked down both offshoots of the tunnel. "We need to—"

Nickie grunted and doubled over as the Gorafrex's drumbeat blasted through the tunnel toward them. It echoed from every direction, making it impossible to tell where they needed to go. "Clubhouse," Emily said, whipping out her keys. She grabbed Nickie's from her sister's back pocket and held the coin out for her. "Let's go."

All three of them pressed their thumbs against the imprint and disappeared.

Nickie staggered out of their arms in the Clubhouse and went straight to the futon to sit. "Oh, man. It's so much worse when that stupid thing's nearby."

"Yeah, I bet. Better in here, though." Emily walked across the room to grab the iron orb she'd put on the shelf, then she stopped and gazed around. "Looks like you guys put together a little arsenal before the party."

"We needed to be ready." Laura glanced at Nickie, who nodded and rubbed her forehead. Laura joined Emily at the bookshelf. "I think we're a lot better prepared than last time."

"Yeah, no kidding." Emily took in the items on the shelf —both of the iron orbs; the iron lance; the Velikan Engineer's oversized socket wrench; and a pair of fingerless leather gloves. "What are these?"

"Those are for you." Laura nodded, and Emily picked the gloves up off the shelf. "Figured you might want your fingers free for spellcasting or…I don't really know everything about how that works with rings instead of wands, yet."

"No one's blaming you for that, Laura."

"Those gloves are really good, though. I've used them to handle a good number of…feisty creatures, I guess. Haven't gotten bitten yet when I wear these."

Emily shot her a confused glance. "I'm gonna let that feisty-creature part go for now." She slipped on the gloves and flexed her fingers. "What about the metal plates in the middle?" Stretching out her hands, she studied the squares of metal attached to each glove's palm.

"I figured, if you timed it right, a simple binding spell with the iron string thing would give you extra leverage before you throw the slingshot."

"Hey, I really like that name. Slingshot. Might use it."

Laura chuckled wryly. "Do what feels right, I guess."

Emily looked at her and smiled softly. "Thanks, Laura. You put some thought into these."

"I'm sorry, Em. About what I said this morning."

"Apology accepted." Emily gave her a thumbs-up and laughed at her bare thumb poking up out of the leather glove.

Nickie stood from the futon, took a deep breath, and bent beside it to open her guitar case on the low coffee table. "I'm glad you guys got that over with. Now I really think we should get back out there and do what we came to do. My brains are fed up with being bashed around inside my head."

Emily grabbed the iron sphere from the shelf and paused. "You goin' with lance or socket wrench?"

Laura's hand shot out for the lance, and she lifted it out in front of her before setting the butt of it onto the ground. "Iron. Putting that thing back in its prison comes first, right? I'll take our shot at that before anything else."

"Okee dokee." Emily walked back toward the center of the Clubhouse and stared at Nickie. "Nice setup. But…you think goin' into this thing with your Strat and a portable amp is the best choice for a Gorafrex fight?"

Nickie stood and straightened her shoulders, then grabbed the handle on the top of the miniature amplifier. "I've been practicing."

"Right, but—"

"A different kind of magic." Nickie winked at her, and Laura stepped up to join them.

Em grinned. "Queen, right?"

Nickie winked. "Bad joke, I know."

"All right…" Laura stood in the middle of the three. "Out of the Clubhouse, then another transport bubble. I'll take care of that one. Make sure you visualize the energy core, but it has to be the one under the street in the neighborhood. Got it?"

"Yep."

"Ready to go."

Laura nodded. "Let's go do our thing, then." They thumbed the coins on their keyrings and disappeared.

The moment they returned to the tunnel, still lit by Laura's glowing light, the Gorafrex's drums hit them.

Nickie gasped and shut her eyes. The opalescent transport bubble bloomed on Laura's ring, grew in front of them, and both Nickie's sisters helped her gently inside. "Think of the core," Laura shouted.

Then they were gone.

CHAPTER THIRTY-ONE

The minute the bubble popped, they found themselves in a half-lit chamber identical to the one where they'd found the first energy core; only, this one had two other women in it, and one of them had a murdering, bodiless being inside of her.

The resounding silence when the Gorafrex's drumbeat cut out was deafening. The woman who'd accosted Emily, the one with matted brown hair and the tattered dress, whipped her head toward them. "I cannot be stopped," she hissed.

In front of her, the Gorafrex's next victim knelt between her and the energy core. Her head was thrown back, eyes wide, mouth open as she breathed heavily but seemed frozen. A strangled moan escaped her, but that was it.

Emily glanced at Laura and mouthed, 'Vanessa.'

Nickie set the amp on the stone floor and switched it on. She gripped her pick and faced the Gorafrex inside the human woman. "Wanna bet?" She strummed the first chord, and her sisters jumped away from the amp as sound exploded through the chamber.

The possessed woman hissed and focused her attention on Vanessa. Rapid drumming picked up once more as the Gorafrex raised its host's hand. At the same time, Nickie launched into the chord progression of the lullaby their dad sung every night until they told him they were too old for lullabies.

For a second, the Gorafrex didn't notice, then the drums faded and the host swiveled her head to glare at Nickie. "You've played that song before." The woman's voice echoed in the chamber almost as loud as the quick, embellished notes from Nickie's Strat. "It almost ruined you." The Gorafrex cocked its head and sniffed at the air. "You would risk the same again, now that I know your scent?"

Nickie kept playing, staring at the woman harboring the murderous creature. She struck another chord, much louder this time, and when she started the lullaby over, her fingers flew.

Laura glanced at Emily and dipped her head, indicating the other side of the chamber. Her sister nodded and started circling around the Gorafrex, whose head kept twitching as it studied the witch playing the oldest, most dangerous spell it knew.

Nickie stepped forward, and the Gorafrex roared. "No!" The possessed woman lunged at the kneeling Vanessa—suspended helplessly by the creature's magic—and raised her hand. The drumming started up again.

Yet, Nickie didn't react to the sound. She didn't hear it at all as she played the one song her ancestors had utilized to lock the vicious being away ages ago.

The woman's eyes flashed a brilliant silver, and Vanessa screamed. From the center of the redheaded witch's chest rose a thin silver filament. It wavered in the air for a second, then elongated and grew, reaching toward the ancient energy core.

"Emily!" Laura shouted.

The youngest Hadstrom sister already had the same thought. She pressed the small round circle in the iron orb and grabbed the released chain with her other hand. A copper light flashed below her glove, binding the thread there, and she hurled the orb at the woman drawing Vanessa's lifeforce out of her and into the energy core.

The odd weapon did exactly as she'd practiced. A blast of magic propelled it in the blink of an eye. It wrapped around the host's neck, eliciting a sharp choke, then spun round and round, pinning the woman's arms to her sides in crisscrossing silver lines.

The host threw her head back and roared. The chamber around them trembled with the sound, fueled by Nickie's constant music. The minute the iron orb stopped, Emily gave it a quick tug and pulled it taut. "Oh, my god, I did it. Laura, I think now's your—"

A growling, rumbling chuckle rose from the host's throat, like a thousand voices in one. "You try so hard," the ancient voice seethed; it didn't belong to the human anymore.

"Wait." Laura stared at the glowing silver filaments

rising from Vanessa's chest. Dozens of them darted this way and that, growing longer, reaching outward toward the core's clear cylinder. "We're missing something. It's about to power the thing anyway." She glanced at Emily. "We have to stop *that*," she shouted, pointing at Vanessa's lifeforce magic being drawn out of her.

"What?"

"We don't have all the—"

A blinding flash flared from where the first tendril of magic touched the energy core. The chamber trembled, and the Gorafrex cackled with its thousand ancient voices.

Laura whipped out her keys and thumbed the coin. The moment she appeared in the Clubhouse, she dropped the lance—useless when they didn't have everything they needed—and leapt toward the bookshelf. She grabbed the Velika and nearly dropped it, but she tightened her grip even as she thumped the coin again and reappeared in the chamber. Without missing a beat, she stormed the energy core, swung the wrench with all the strength she had, and brought it cracking up into the closest part of the cylinder.

The force of that blow vibrated up her arms and into her shoulders, but she kept her grip on the wrench. The energy core spit a violent spray of green sparks, hissing and spewing, and the ancient blue magic shot up the cylinder in crackling streaks. An actual crack ran up the side of the clear structure, and the whole thing started to crumble.

The magic draining out of Vanessa's chest slithered back into her just as the first shower of shattered energy core rained down. Some silver threads had already entered the cylinder, though, and appeared to activate some part of it. A high-pitched whine rose from the base set into the chamber floor, and a blue light flashed from it, strobing faster and faster.

The Gorafrex growled and writhed within the Emily's silvery net. The chamber shook, and the woman host's flailing snapped the iron thread from its place inside the orb. The orb fell to the ground with a metallic ring and rolled behind the shattered energy core.

"No, no, no!" Emily couldn't pull her end of the iron thread fast enough to draw it tight, and the Gorafrex shook its host's body and slipped free of the thin chain binding.

The creature stepped out of the looped pile at its feet and hissed at the witches. "Never again," it spat.

The drums rattled, and a shimmering aura like some swirling, gelatinous thing grew around the woman's body. A second later, the Gorafrex shot up out of its human host and hurtled across the cavern. Nickie's music cut out with a grating shriek, and the aura of glowing energy darted over her head and into the tunnel beyond.

The human it had inhabited for at least the last five days—who would wake up soon only to find that the tiny, pea-sized brain at the top of her spine had now awakened her to the most powerful magic of any being on this giant ship they called Earth—slumped to the floor and lay still. Vanessa did the same right after her.

"We need to get out of here," Laura shouted.

Emily groaned and cut the iron chain from her glove with a severing spell.

Nickie grabbed up her amp and ran to the two unconscious women. A huge puff of dust and small pebbles rained down from the chamber ceiling, and Laura summoned a transport bubble around the women on the floor. Just as the bubble took them all from the ancient underground chamber, the rest of the energy core split, and its jagged fragments smashed down onto the floor where they'd just stood.

Her phone dinged, waking her. Emily rolled over in bed. Her vision was blurry for a few seconds before she saw it was almost 9:00 a.m.

John had texted her: *'How's Nickie?'*

She rubbed her face, blinked heavily, and rolled onto her back to text a reply.

'Better. We got what she needed. Just took a long time. Again, sorry we weren't able to come back.'

'No worries. I like Chuck. Nathan's...interesting.'

She laughed and shook her head as her fingers moved across the keyboard.

'Still on for tomorrow?'

'Duh.'

'Good.'

With a sigh, she set her phone back down on the bedside table and stared at the ceiling. "I bet Nathan's more interesting now that he's heard the whole story. Laura did not like that part. Still, she's probably nowhere near as freaked out as that woman whose peabrain is now making her feel like someone drugged her…for the rest of her life." She closed her eyes. "Yep. Everyone says we have to leave the awakened humans alone and let them figure it out for themselves. Doesn't mean I have to like it."

Knowing she wouldn't be able to go back to sleep, she pushed herself up and glanced at the one iron orb she still had. "Gotta figure out how to make that chain stronger. Or at least whatever it is Laura thinks we're still missing. 'Cause that obviously did not work." Emily glanced out her bedroom window. "I sound like Laura now, talking to myself."

Outside, a flock of huge grackles swarmed across Pressler Street, squawking and shrieking their noisy cry wherever they went.

"Yeah, yeah. I know. We're still not done." Emily threw the covers off her lap, slid out of bed, and headed for the door. Speed popped his head up from where he lay on the foot of the bed and snorted. "Come on, buddy. Coffee first."

The trio of witches are struggling with the tasks before them and the Gorafrex is still on the loose. When the grackles fall out of the sky and have lost their voices, the women know things are very wrong. Time to step up the game and learn some new tricks to put the Gorafrex away in Spellbound Magic.

Get sneak peeks, exclusive giveaways, behind the scenes content, and more.
PLUS you'll be notified of special **one day only fan pricing** on new releases.

Sign up today to get free stories.

CLICK HERE

or visit: https://marthacarr.com/read-free-stories/

AUTHOR NOTES - MARTHA CARR

DECEMBER 6, 2019

Most of you know that I moved into my dream house last September. The house that Yumfuck Tiberius Troll built. And the entire neighborhood has turned out to be its own secret garden. My small piece of Austin is tucked away, near open fields but only fifteen minutes from downtown. Still, there's not a lot of here… well, here, yet. Turns out, that's okay. I have a very special kind of neighbors living around me. They like doing things – all the time.

This is a new neighborhood – old timers are anyone who's been here for three years. They talk about *all* the changes they've seen like a generation has passed. The houses are filled with all kinds of people, mostly in their 30's with a diversity that enriches the place.

But that's just the start of what makes this place so unique and I'm staying till I'm dead and gone. It's a spark, an openness that is rare and wonderful. First hint there was something was the first time I walked the good dog, Lois Lane up to the mailboxes and a neighbor, Nicole, was standing in front of her new house of about an hour waving wildly for me to come over and say hello. She quickly spit out that they just closed on their house and to come back on Saturday, there would be a party.

Didn't take long till I heard about the clubs. There's a cooking club (more of an eat and drink club), a crafts club, a poker club, a running club, a Bunko club, a fantasy football club. A neighbor who teaches gun safety taught a bunch of us how to handle guns correctly. It was posted on our Facebook neighborhood group and open to anyone who wanted to know. I wanted to hang out and I figured the more knowledge the better – even if it's just for the writing. I found out shooting a gun is not as easy as it looks.

Then the HOA started hosting parties. An adult Easter egg hunt with liquor and candy for prizes as well as a children's hunt the next day. Food trucks and an outdoor movie on the first Friday of every month. What is this place? And how did I get so lucky?

Best part was yet to come. The oft talked about but not quite finished amenity center finally opened in July – a resort-style pool, full gym (that's right – full-size, not fun size), an outdoor area with a firepit and indoor area with couches, large screen TVs, kitchen, and pool table. I think a good portion of that jump in sales for hard seltzer was from my neighbors hanging out at the pool. Frankly, I've been referring to the pool as a living room with water after seeing how many adults like to just stand in the water and hold a drink. I passed a neighbor on the way in one day and casually said, "How's it going?" He said, "Living the good life," and sounded a little choked up. I totally get it dude.

Last weekend, the HOA doubled down and had an adults only cocktail hour at the pool with a neighbor acting as a deejay and then the next night had two bands and a bar and food truck. I see my neighbors over at the amenity center so much I think of it as the commons and our houses as our dorm rooms.

One more hurrah came my way this week. My front yard was named October's Yard of the Month, complete with a sign in the front, my picture in the newsletter and a gift card to Home Depot. That troll has been magical for me from the start – and this dream house, dream neighborhood is just one more piece of wonderful proof. More adventures to follow.

MIDWEST MAGIC CHRONICLES
SOUL STONE MAGE
THE FAIRHAVEN CHRONICLES

OTHER BOOKS BY JUDITH BERENS

OTHER BOOKS BY MARTHA CARR

OTHER BOOKS BY MICHAEL ANDERLE

JOIN THE TERRANAVIS UNIVERSE FAN GROUP ON FACEBOOK!

JOIN THE PEABRAIN SOCIETY GROUP ON FACEBOOK!

www.ingramcontent.com/pod-product-compliance
Lightning Source LLC
Chambersburg PA
CBHW050233110726

47898CB00007B/2133